The Stolen Years

By

Ernest Barrett

Copyright © Ernest Barrett 2015
This book is sold subject to the condition that it shall not, by way of trade or otherwise, be lent, resold, hired out, or otherwise circulated without the publisher's prior consent in any form of binding or cover other than that in which it is published and without a similar condition including this condition being imposed on the subsequent publisher.
The moral right of Ernest Barrett has been asserted.
ISBN-13: 978-1512111897
ISBN-10: 1512111899

DEDICATION

I would like to dedicate this book to all children who are taken into care or are adopted.

CONTENTS

Chapter 1 .... *1*
Chapter 2 .... *9*
Chapter 3 .... *28*
Chapter 4 .... *38*
Chapter 5 .... *48*
Chapter 6 .... *71*
Chapter 7 .... *86*
Chapter 8 .... *112*
Chapter 9 .... *137*
Chapter 10 .... *153*
Chapter 11 .... *174*
Chapter 12 .... *190*
Chapter 13 .... *211*
Chapter 14 .... *231*

Chapter 1

Ronald Malling, a five foot ten, heavily built man, stretched his arms out wide before giving a deep sigh; he had a strong feeling of well-being as he looked up at the clear blue sky.

'It's going to be a fine day,' he muttered to himself as he waited for his wife Marion to come out of the front door of their neat bungalow which was situated on the outskirts of Lincoln in the village of Langworth. He paused for a few seconds as he cast his eyes around the well-kept garden before locking the door. There was a contented smile on his round face as he followed Marion to the car which was standing in the driveway; opening the car door he climbed in and settled his large frame behind the steering wheel. After securing his seatbelt he turned to his wife who was struggling with hers.

'Can you manage to fasten it my love?' he enquired, a questioning expression on his face.

Marion shuffled her ample backside in the seat for a few seconds before carefully fastening her seatbelt and making herself comfortable, a lock of slightly greying hair falling over her blue eyes as she nodded her head and assured him, 'I'm all right Ron.'

'Right we'll get off then,' her husband declared as he started the engine and guided the car carefully out of the driveway and on to the road; he gave a wave to his neighbour Bill who was in the process of mowing his lawn as they accelerated away.

They were going on a long awaited holiday to the Bahamas. Fifty-three year old Ronald and his friend Alan Frost were partners in a small printing firm; after spending years building the business up they had finally reached a position where they could relax a little.

'You go and get yourself a good holiday Ron,' his partner had told him. 'When you come back it will be my turn.'

Ronald nodded in agreement before going home and telling Marion, who had just got over the traumatic experience of a hysterectomy. After spending half an hour looking carefully through the brochure she chose a hotel in the Bahamas.

'The area looks idyllic Ron,' she enthused as she took in the blue sea and the palm trees.

'If that's where you want to go my love, then that is where we are going,' he told her as he reached out, picked up the phone and booked one week's holiday.

The couple had one daughter, twenty year old Rebecca; she was in her second year of studying for a degree in fashion and design at university in London. She and her boyfriend Joseph Melstrom, who was working for a computer firm in London, were staying together in a flat in the capital; it wasn't the ideal situation as far as her parents were concerned, they would much rather she had married before moving in with Joseph, but after meeting the young man and seeing that he was a 'decent lad', as her dad had put it, they had reluctantly accepted the arrangement.

Ron and Marion had come to the conclusion that it would be a good idea to take the holiday while Rebecca was away from home. Ronald took his eyes off the road for few seconds, raised his arm and glanced at his wristwatch as they drove carefully through the village.

'It's eight thirty,' he told her as he put his foot down on the accelerator, adding that they should be at Gatwick Airport well before four thirty, which was the time of their flight.

The journey to Newark where they would join the A1 was really enjoyable as they made their way across the open countryside. The sun was shining from a predominantly blue sky as the spacious Volvo sped smoothly on its way. Three quarters of an hour later they turned on to the dual carriageway. Ronald smiled inwardly as he told himself that, at last he could get moving. Marion laid her head back on the head rest, closed her eyes and listened to the relaxing music that was emanating from the radio. Ronald was humming to himself along with the rendition as the car sped along in the outside lane at 60 mph. He was just about to pass a van which was on the lane inside him when it suddenly slewed out in front of him.

'What the hell?' he spluttered as he banged his foot down on the brakes and took evasive action – to no avail. The driver of a car that was following him braked sharply to avoid smashing into his rear end. Marion screamed as they rammed into the van; there was a look of horror on her husband's face as the car hit the barrier that ran along the central reservation, flipped over on its roof as it rebounded, and rolled onto the inside lane of the busy freeway, where heavy vehicles were making their way at a more steady pace.

Alastair Murray took his right hand off the steering wheel and ran the palm of his hand over the short stubby bristles on his head. He had been on the road over four hours, having set off from Glasgow at five thirty a.m. and he was beginning to feel the strain. The drumming of the heavy vehicle's tyres on the tarmac of the busy A1 was almost sending him to sleep; he was brought suddenly to his senses as he saw a car on the outside lane collide with a van, then hit the central barrier before rolling over and sliding on its roof across the carriageway; eventually finishing in the inside lane in front of his vehicle.

'Good grief…' he growled as he put his full weight on the foot brake in an attempt to avoid a collision. To no avail.

The articulated lorry slammed into the car, knocking it to one side. The couple never knew what hit them as the rest of the traffic swerved to miss the wrecked car.

A few minutes later the sound of sirens could be heard as the police and the ambulance swerved their way through the halted traffic to the scene of the tragedy. The police put a blockade up as the ambulance men wrenched open the doors of the battered vehicle.

Forty-five year old John Dicer's face screwed up as he got down on his knees and looked at the two battered bodies hanging in their seatbelts. He reached inside the car and felt the wrist of the woman whose eyes were half-closed, he could just make out a faint beat as he held his fingers on her pulse.

'I reckon this lady is still alive Alan,' he informed his partner as he reached inside the car and struggled to unfasten the seatbelt which was holding her up.

Alan Rushman had opened the driver's side and pushed back the male driver who was hanging in the straps, his battered face dripping blood. After thoroughly checking him he muttered, 'I'm afraid this one is dead.'

Seeing that his partner was struggling to free the badly injured woman, he made his way round to the other side of the car to help him.

'Right John, I'll hold her up while you unfasten the seatbelt,' he offered as he got down on his knees and squeezed himself under her, before reaching up with his brawny arms, taking the woman's weight and lifting her in order to loosen the straps.

'Hold it there Alan,' wheezed John as he reached out and unclipped the seatbelt.

A couple of minutes later as they were easing the woman's body out of the car, two police officers arrived on the scene.

'What have we got then?' enquired one of the two six-footers as they approached the sweating ambulance men.

Alan ran his fingers through his thick dark hair as he turned to the officer in question; he informed him that one of the two occupants in the car, a male, was dead and that the one that they had just taken out of the car, a female, was badly injured.

PC James Anders stroked his chin as he and his

partner Constable Desmond Riley, who had a note book in his hand and was taking notes, surveyed the scene as they walked round the smashed up car.

He turned to a group of drivers that had gathered as the ambulance crew removed the two bodies from the car, swiftly placed them in the ambulance and drove off at speed, sirens wailing.

'Did anyone see what happened?' he put to them.

One of them, a short stocky man, piped up. 'Yes, I did. I was behind this car when the accident happened.'

PC Riley, pen in hand, asked him, 'And your name is?'

'Albert Jenson.'

'Can you tell me how the incident occurred in your own words?'

'Well,' the man began, 'I was driving what you might call a safe distance behind the Volvo in the outside lane when the red van.'

Jenson paused for a moment and pointed at the vehicle in question before going on.

'It was on the inner lane and seemed to swerve in front of the Volvo.'

He gave a shrug of his shoulders and nodded towards the body of the driver of the car that was being placed in the ambulance. 'He didn't stand a chance.'

The policeman turned to the other drivers that were crowded round him.

'Which one of you is the lorry driver?' he enquired, running his eyes over the group.

The tall gangly figure of Alastair Murray stepped in

front of him and told him that he was the driver.

'Can you describe what happened?' the police officer put to him.

Murray scratched the back of his neck for a few seconds as he thought over his reply. 'I was cruising along smoothly when I saw the red van which was travelling in the inside lane ahead of me, suddenly swerve to the right, straight into the path of the Volvo; this in turn slammed into the van then into the barrier before rolling over and finishing in front of me.'

He stopped for a moment and took a deep breath before continuing in his broad Scottish accent. 'I couldnay avoid the Volvo!' he exclaimed, shaking his head vigorously.

The policeman chewed on the end of the pen for a few seconds, he had a deep frown on his forehead as he turned and approached the van driver who was still sat in his van looking down between his legs, holding his head in his hands.

'Can I have your name sir?' he asked.

The man looked up at him, blood from a cut on the top of his balding head trickling down his forehead; the injury was probably caused by his head hitting the windscreen, which was smashed.

'James Ronson,' he mumbled.

'Is it true that your van swerved towards the car in question?' he asked a little sharply.

'Yes it's true,' he replied, an anguished expression on his face.

'What exactly happened?' enquired the policeman pointedly.

Ronson shrugged his shoulders, as he shook his

head slowly from side to side.

'I… I'm not sure,' he replied falteringly. 'One minute I was driving along comfortably, then suddenly I was trying to pull the van back on to a straight course. The next thing I knew the car had hit me.'

He paused for few seconds before adding somewhat dejectedly, 'I must have dropped off to sleep.'

After checking that except for the cut and a bruise on his cheekbone, which was blackening by the minute, he hadn't received any other injuries, the police officer informed him, 'I will have to place you under arrest for suspected dangerous driving Mr Ronson.' Reaching out, he took hold of his arm and led him to the police car.

By this time heavy vehicles had arrived to take away the two damaged vehicles.

PC Anders turned to the two witnesses, telling them that they may be called to give evidence in the future. After taking their addresses he dismissed them. They and the other drivers that had been standing around went back to their respective vehicles and one by one drove off. Ten minutes later the traffic was moving smoothly; except for a large oil stain on the highway, it was just as if nothing had happened. The two policemen made their way back to Lincoln Headquarters with the man that they had arrested who was duly charged and placed in custody.

Chapter 2

It was three o'clock on Saturday afternoon and Rebecca Malling was just getting ready to go out shopping in London with her boyfriend Joseph. She was humming to herself as she ran the comb through her long dark hair in front of the mirror on the wall in the bathroom of the flat where they were staying together. Suddenly the sharp ring of the doorbell cut through her humming.

'I'll get it,' called out her boyfriend from the kitchen.

A few seconds went by before Joseph could be heard opening the door. A policewoman was standing in front of him.

'Yes, can I help you?' he enquired.

The policewoman asked him if she could speak to a Rebecca Malling.

There was a pause for a moment before he told her, 'Hold on a second, I'll go and get her.'

Rebecca was just coming out of the bathroom into the hallway, a deep frown on her forehead, as Joseph approached her.

'It's the police for you,' he muttered, a little secretively.

'Police?' she mouthed questioningly, before going to the door where the policewoman was waiting to speak to her.

'I'm Rebecca Malling, won't you come in?' she said in a low voice.

The WPC thanked her and followed her into the lounge.

'Now what can I do for you?' enquired Rebecca as she and the policewoman sat on the worn settee.

'I'm afraid I've got some bad news for you Miss Malling regarding your parents,' the solemn-faced young official told her, looking down at her clasped hands.

'Bad news?' queried Rebecca, her brow furrowed. 'What do you mean by bad news, they're not in trouble are they?'

'I'm afraid they've been involved in an accident,' was the blunt reply.

'An accident!' she exclaimed, a horrified expression on her face. 'Are they hurt?'

'All I can tell you is that they were involved in a car accident at around ten a.m. this morning on the A1. According to the information that I have received, your father has been killed and your mother is badly injured,' the young woman said feelingly as Rebecca, her face chalk white with shock, burst into tears.

'What's the matter Rebecca?' enquired Joseph, as he entered the room and put a comforting arm round her shoulder when he saw how upset she was.

'My mum and dad have had an accident in the car and my dad has been killed,' she said chokingly as she placed her face in her hands and sobbed uncontrollably.

'What a terrible thing to happen when they were just going on their holiday,' whispered Joseph feelingly in her ear as he gave her his handkerchief.

The policewoman in the meantime had got to her feet and was making for the door.

'I'll be going now Miss Malling, I'm sorry to have brought you such bad news,' she told the upset young woman.

Rebecca nodded her head and dabbed her eyes as the WPC went through the door.

Joseph placed his arm round her shoulders and comforted her.

'I'll have to ring my uncle and tell him of the accident,' Rebecca mumbled into the handkerchief.

Picking up her small handbag she took out a book and leafed through it. 'Here we are,' she said before reaching for the phone and ringing the number; after a couple of rings it was answered.

'Hello, Brian Malling here.'

'Uncle Brian, Rebecca here. I've got some terrible news for you.'

She paused for a moment before telling him, her voice breaking as she did so. 'Mum and Dad have been involved in an accident. Dad is dead.'

'Don't talk silly Rebecca. Who's told you that?'

'The police have just informed me. They told me that they were involved in an accident this morning on the A1.' She stopped for a second to blow her nose before going on to tell him, 'They were going on holiday.' There was a deathly silence from Brian as the information sank in.

'Well I'll be…' he spluttered into the mouthpiece, before asking her: 'Are you coming down?'

'Yes as soon as I can sort it out with the head of the university,' she replied.

'When will you be coming?' enquired Brian.

'Probably Monday morning,' she told him.

'You can stay here with me.'

'Thank you Uncle, but I've decided to stay at our home in Langworth, I will have a few things to sort out,' she said firmly.

The rest of the weekend seemed like a month as visions of her mum and dad passed endlessly through her mind. Joseph tried his utmost to comfort her, to no avail.

It was Monday morning; Rebecca knocked on the door of the head of the university.

'Come in,' a gruff voice called out.

She opened the door, and walked in.

He was studying a document. It was on the desk in front of him.

'Now what can I do for you young lady?' he enquired, looking into her hazel eyes.

'I wish to apply for some time off to settle some personal business Mr Hinton,' she told him in a soft voice.

Jonathan Hinton folded his arms and leaned back in his chair, a deep frown creasing his forehead as his brown eyes bored into her red rimmed ones. 'Rebecca

Malling isn't it?' he put to her.

'Yes sir,' she replied, nodding her head.

He clasped his fingers in front of him and chewed on his bottom lip for a few seconds before informing her in a serious tone of voice, 'This is a most unusual request at this stage of your course. Have you a good reason?'

She looked down at the floor and took a deep breath before telling him, 'My mother and father were involved in a car accident on Saturday morning.'

He sat bolt upright in his chair.

'Were they injured?' he enquired, a concerned expression on his face.

'My mother was badly injured and my dad was killed,' she explained falteringly, tears rolling down her cheeks.

Springing out of his chair he strode round the desk and placed his arm comfortingly around her shoulders. 'Never mind my dear, we'll help you all we can,' he declared in a soft voice.

Opening the office door he stuck his head out and called out loudly, 'Miss Johnson!'

A middle aged woman wearing thick rimmed glasses and her hair tied in a bun at the back of her head came rushing out of a small office next door.

'Yes Mr Hinton?' she said, a questioning frown on her forehead as she entered his office.

'Can you make out a form for leave of absence for this young lady?' he instructed her.

'How long shall I make it out for Mr Hinton?'

'As long as it takes,' he replied.

He turned to Rebecca and told her to go along

with Miss Johnson, explaining to her that she would make out the necessary forms.

'Thank you Mr Hinton, you've been a great help,' she replied as she turned and followed the secretary to her office.

'Sit down Rebecca,' said Miss Johnson in a kindly voice, pointing to a chair that stood in front of the desk. Miss Johnson took a seat opposite her on the other side of the desk. Pulling out a drawer, she rummaged in it for a few seconds.

'Here we are,' she declared as she placed a sheet of A4 in the typewriter.

She paused for a moment before requesting her full name.

'Rebecca Malling,' she told her nervously.

'You don't have to be afraid of me dear,' Miss Johnson said smilingly.

Rebecca nodded and smiled back, assuring her, 'I'm not nervous it's just that I've received some bad news over the weekend.'

'Oh dear,' replied the secretary. 'And what would that be?'

Rebecca looked down at her clasped hands for a moment before telling her, 'My mother has been injured and my father has been killed in a car accident.'

'Oh I am sorry,' declared Miss Johnson as she put the final touches to the letter.

Reaching once more into the drawer she took out an envelope and placed the form in it before handing it to Rebecca.

'I hope everything goes on all right for you my

dear,' she confided as she handed her the envelope before enquiring, 'by the way when are you setting off for home?'

'I am going to catch the train this afternoon,' Rebecca informed her.

Thanking the secretary she got to her feet and turned to go through the door. Her hand was on the door knob when Miss Johnson asked her if she had any transport to take her to her digs which were on the other side of London. She shook her head.

'Hold on a minute Rebecca I'll just have a word with Mister Hinton.'

Reaching out, she picked the phone up and spoke into it. After a couple of nods at the receiver she told Rebecca, 'Mr Hinton says it's okay to have a lift with one of the college cars.'

'Thank you Miss Johnson you've been very helpful,' she whispered a little emotionally as she went through the door.

'Er, Helen, my name's Helen,' the older woman told her smilingly.

Rebecca closed the door behind her and set off along the lengthy corridor as she made her way to the exit, envelope in hand. She took a deep breath as she stepped out on to the large car park. A man approached her.

'Are you the young lady who needs a lift to her digs?' he enquired.

Rebecca smiled and nodded her head.

'This way,' he told her, pointing across the car park.

After giving him the address, they were on their way through the busy London streets. Fifteen minutes later he stopped the car outside the block of flats where she and Joseph were staying. Climbing out of the car she smiled her thanks, then with a wave of his hand and a, 'Best of luck,' he drove off. After entering the flat she phoned Joseph and informed him that she had been given permission to take enough time off from university to complete her affairs regarding her parents.

'If you hang on for a couple of hours Becky I'll go with you!' he exclaimed.

'No Joseph,' she replied firmly. 'I don't know how long I'm going to be and you can't leave your job.'

Rebecca lost no time in quickly gathering her belongings, enjoying a quick sandwich and a cup of coffee before setting off to the railway station, which was close by.

Using her university pass she acquired a cheap rate ticket to Lincoln. Half an hour later she was boarding the train that would take her to the cold empty house that once was a happy home. The sun was high in the sky as she made the journey across the English countryside; her mind was in turmoil as the thought of the accident threatened to overwhelm her. The long journey seemed never ending as the fields of corn and cattle flashed by, a sight that would normally enthral her, but with the terrible pain she was feeling in her breast, it was as nothing.

Eventually the three towers of Lincoln Cathedral hove into view. She gave a heartfelt sigh as she got to her feet, and reached up to the luggage rack and took down her case. A few minutes later she was stepping out on to the station platform. After checking out of the station, she made her way to the bus station where she boarded a bus that was going to the hospital. Ten minutes later she was jumping off at the bus stop that was only thirty yards away from the hospital entrance.

Pushing open the glass swing doors, she approached the long reception counter. A young woman addressed her.

'Can I help you?' she said, her freckled face creasing in a smile.

Rebecca explained to her that her mother had been involved in an accident and that she was in the hospital. After giving her mother's name, the receptionist went over to a computer, and tapped the keys before coming back to her.

'You want ward three on the second floor. It's the emergency ward,' she explained, pointing to a lift which was situated on the other side of the large room.

Rebecca, case in hand, walked across to the lift just as the sliding door opened and an elderly lady in a wheelchair was pushed out by one of the nurses. Standing to one side she let the wheelchair come out before stepping inside the lift. The door automatically closed when she pressed the button for the third floor. A few seconds later she walked out of the lift and made her way along the corridor checking the wards on either side as she went.

A nurse coming towards her from the opposite direction noticed the perplexed expression on her face.

'Can I help you?' she asked, a friendly smile on her round face.

Rebecca nodded her head before telling her that she was looking for her mother, Marion Malling, who was in intensive care.

'You'll be wanting ward four my dear,' the short well-endowed nurse told her in a Scottish accent, adding after giving it a little thought, 'come on I'll take you there.'

Rebecca nodded her thanks and followed her along the corridor. A few seconds later she stopped outside the door of one of the wards.

'Here you are my dear,' she told her in a low voice as she led the way into the ward.

She stopped at a bed that was curtained off. Pulling back the curtain she told Rebecca concernedly, in a low voice, 'Don't stay for too long, she's very ill.'

Rebecca thanked her before approaching the bed where her mother was laying, her eyes closed. There were tears in the young woman's eyes as she leaned over and kissed her gently on the cheek, telling her in a quiet voice, 'I love you Mum.'

Marion's eyes fluttered open as she heard her daughter's voice.

'Rebecca?' she whispered questioningly.

'Yes Mum I'm here,' she replied comfortingly.

'I've got something to tell you,' her mum murmured, almost inaudibly.

Rebecca placed her ear close to her mum's lips.

'Go on Mum I'm listening,'

Marion took a deep breath before telling her, in a forced tone of voice, 'There are some forms in a tin box in my bedroom.'

She paused for a moment, her face screwing up in pain before carrying on.

'Your dad and me adopted you when you were four years old,' she breathed. Then, taking another deep breath she went on. 'We didn't know who your parents were when we took you in. But we've always loved you as our own.'

Rebecca's brow was deeply furrowed as she absorbed the 'confession' that her mother had just told her. *Is my mum hallucinating?* she asked herself.

'I, I can't believe that Mum,' she gasped, looking down at the bruised pale face on the pillow.

Marion's eyes closed for few seconds before fluttering open again.

'It's true my dear,' she assured her before going on to explain. 'Your dad and me couldn't have children.' Her voice was gradually fading as she spoke.

'We'll talk about that when you get better Mum,' Rebecca murmured in her ear.

Marion smiled weakly before arching her back and taking a deep breath. Then with a long sigh she sank down, her eyes gazing unseeing at the young woman by her side.

Rebecca sat up straight, a shocked expression on her face.

'Nurse,' she called out in a loud voice. There was a note of urgency in it.

A young nurse opened the curtain.

'Is everything all right?' she enquired.

'It's my mum,' replied Rebecca shakily, as she nodded toward her mother.

The nurse approached the bed and bent over the stricken woman; she had a sombre expression on her face as she turned to the young woman. 'I'm afraid she's passed away my dear,' she intoned, shaking her head.

Tears rolled down Rebecca's face as she leaned over her mum and gave her a kiss.

'I love you Mum,' she whispered feelingly, before turning away from the bed and walking out of the ward, quietly sobbing.

It was a more sober Rebecca who disembarked from the bus when it arrived back at Langworth. Giving a deep sigh she walked down the drive to the front door of the bungalow; taking out the key that her dad had given her to use when they were out, she opened the door and stepped inside. Tears welled up in her eyes as they settled on a large photograph of her parents that stood alongside the telephone on the polished top table in the hallway. There was a haunting silence as she walked into the large lounge and sat down on the settee, still dabbing her eyes with her handkerchief as she looked around the large room. After a few minutes had gone by she got to her feet and made her way into what was her parents' bedroom. Going over to the bedside cabinet, she sat down on the edge of the bed, opened the top drawer and rummaged through it, looking for any object that would bring back for a few seconds, the closeness that she had with her mum and dad; under the long drawer were two cupboards, leaning over she checked the nearest one. It consisted of one shelf, upon which was the black metal box that her mother had told her of; there was a questioning look on her face as she reached inside the cupboard and lifted it out. Placing it on the bed she lifted the lid. Three large envelopes containing documents confronted her. Inquisitively she carefully leafed through them; the first one contained her parents' marriage lines. Another had copies of a few documents appertaining to the bungalow. The third one, which was quite thick, had nothing written on the front of it. Laying her head back on the pillow she opened it and took out the folded documents that were inside it. On the front of them was written in large words. 'Adoption Papers'. Underneath this heading there were instructions to destroy the papers, which obviously her 'parents' had ignored. She opened out the documents and carefully ran her eyes over the first one, a questioning expression on her face.

Rebecca sat bolt upright as she absorbed the instruction. She shook her head slowly from side to side as she unfolded the rest of the documents and slowly read them.

There was a look of disbelief on her face as she read the information on the sheets of paper. It told of a four-year-old girl changing hands for the sum of ten thousand pounds. It was dated 1968. It was an agreement for the adoptive parents to pay the sum of two thousand pounds per year for five years. It was signed 'R Malling'.

She sat for a few seconds, her face white with shock as she counted out on her fingers the years indicated.

'That little girl would be about twenty by now,' she muttered to herself.

Her mind was in turmoil when the phone rang, she picked up the receiver.

'Hello!' she exclaimed, in a somewhat husky,

emotional voice.

'Is that Rebecca?' a man's voice enquired.

'Yes,' she replied, nodding her head at the phone.

'Uncle Brian here,' said the voice. 'Are you okay?'

'Yes I'm all right,' she mumbled a little tearfully, before going on to tell him of her mum dying in hospital.

'Well just sit tight Becky,' he told her firmly, 'I'll be with you in twenty minutes.'

Putting the phone down she continued searching through the rest of the documents for any information that would enlighten her with regard to the adoption, to no avail. Suddenly the front door burst open and her Uncle Brian walked in.

'Hi Becky!' he said as he approached and gave her a peck on the cheek.

'Hello Uncle Brian,' she replied a little tearfully.

'Now, now,' he muttered feelingly, placing his arm comfortingly around her shoulders, telling her, 'I'll help you as much as I can.'

'Do you know anything about this?' she asked him, holding out the document that spoke of an adoption.

Brian had a look of disbelief on his face as he ran his eyes over the statement that was written on what looked like official documents.

'I'm afraid I didn't know anything about an adoption,' he told her, shaking his head and telling her: 'Our Ron and Marion didn't mention it to me.'

'The child that my mum and dad adopted would be twenty years old now,' she told him, adding in almost a whisper, 'that's my age.'

Uncle Brian chewed on his bottom lip for a few

seconds as he thought over the implications of what she had said, before repeating with a shake of his head, 'Your dad didn't mention anything to me about you being adopted throughout the years I've known you.'

'Well my mum did tell me that I had been adopted just before she passed away,' she put to him falteringly.

He leaned back in his chair, folded his arms and stroked his chin reflectively as he cast his mind back over the years.

'The first time I set eyes on you was when I came home from Germany.'

He paused for a few seconds his eyes half closed, before going on to tell her, 'I was twenty-five at the time and had just finished six and a half years in the RAF.'

He paused again before carrying on. 'You were just four years old.'

'Where were my mum and dad during the four years?'

He scratched the back of his neck and ran his hand over his balding head before telling her, 'I'm afraid I don't know for certain.'

He reached out, picked up the document and ran his eyes over it again.

'Is the envelope there?' he asked her.

Rebecca picked up the metal box and foraged among the papers that were in it. 'Here it is,' she told him, handing him a stamped envelope.

He studied the post mark carefully. He could just make out the word 'Boston' written across the stamp.

'Mmm,' he murmured, his eyes half closed. 'If I remember rightly our Ron wrote to me from the Boston area when I was in the RAF.'

'My mum told me that I was born in a village named Fishtoft,' she said excitedly.

'That's it. I remember now, Fairview, Woad Lane, Fishtoft,' announced Brian.

After telling her that she should look into it at the Boston offices of Births and Deaths to check the details, he got down to the nitty gritty of organising the funeral of her dead parents; upon making enquiries they were told by the authorities that the funeral would have to wait until after an investigation into the accident had been completed by the police department and the insurance company.

'Where are you going to stay Becky?' her uncle asked her.

She had a solemn expression on her face as she told him that she would be staying at home.

'Are you sure you will be okay staying here?' enquired her uncle, a worried frown on his forehead.

'I'll be all right,' she assured him as he turned to leave.

A few minutes later she waved him off as he reversed the car out of the driveway and drove off.

She walked into the lounge and stood in front of the large mirror that hung over the stone fireplace and studied herself. After a couple of minutes gazing at the unhappy figure in front of her, she took a deep breath and decided to pull herself together.

'There's nothing I can do to change what has happened,' she muttered firmly before turning away, going into the kitchen and making herself a cup of tea.

Taking out a large photograph album from a drawer, she settled down with her cup of tea and carefully went through it. There were a few pictures of her at different ages with her parents. She had a tear in her eye as she turned the pages. She did note one thing, not one of the photos showed her as a baby. She was deep in thought as she slowly closed the album. Her mind was in a whirl as she contemplated the fact that she had probably been adopted. She resolved that she would make enquiries the next day.

Following a restless night tossing and turning, she took a shower; this was followed by a quick breakfast before catching the bus to Boston, where she contacted the department for 'Births and Deaths'. Going up to the long counter, she was approached by a female member of staff.

'Can I help you?' the young woman enquired, a friendly smile on her face.

Rebecca explained to her what had happened regarding her parents' accident and that she had discovered that she may have been adopted.

'Is there any way that I can find out?' she asked her.

The woman's brow was furrowed for a few seconds before coming to a decision.

'I'll have a word with Mr Griffiths and see what we can do,' she told her firmly as she went off to talk to a middle aged balding man who was sat at a desk at the rear of the office.

After listening carefully to what the office worker had to say the heavily built man got to his feet and approached her. He dipped his head slightly and looked at her over his thick rimmed glasses

'Now then young lady what's this all about?' he asked her in a gravelly voice.

Rebecca went carefully through what she had told the young woman.

He stroked his chin as he thought over what she had told him before asking her, 'Can you give me your name and address and your date of birth?'

After she had given it to him, he went over to a large metal cabinet and pulled open one of the long, deep drawers. A few minutes later, after carefully leafing through a thick pack of folders, he drew one of the folders out of the pack and took it to his desk, where he opened it and proceeded to run his eyes down the long list of names. Eventually he came to the end of the list. He sat back in his chair for a couple of seconds and plucked at his bottom lip, his brow deeply furrowed, before getting to his feet and approaching her.

'I'm afraid I can't find any reference of an adoption during the time that you have indicated,' he told her.

She looked him in the eyes, her brow deeply furrowed.

'Does that mean that I wasn't adopted?'

He shook his head; he had a serious expression on his face.

'Not really,' he replied, adding somewhat thoughtfully, 'what it may mean is that you were unlawfully adopted.' He paused for a moment before telling her, 'There is something else puzzling me.'

'What would that be?' she asked him.

'I can't find any reference to your birth under your name.'

She gave a half laugh. 'That's impossible.'

He gave a shrug of his shoulders before telling her that there was another problem.

'Another problem?' she put to him.

'Yes, I'm afraid there is no reference to your date of birth either. Not on the date that you gave me.'

Rebecca was nonplussed as she absorbed what the official had told her.

'Is there anything you can do about it?' she asked him.

The man drummed his fingers on the top of the counter for a few seconds before coming to a decision.

'I will get in touch with the powers that be and inform them of the situation,' he informed her. 'We'll contact you at later date.'

Rebecca thanked him before turning to leave, a puzzled expression on her face.

Chapter 3

It was Monday morning. Chief Inspector Wilberton pushed the door open and stepped into the reception office at Lincoln Police Headquarters.

'Good morning sir,' said Sergeant Bellows, a broad smile on his face as the chief came through the door.

Wilberton gave a smile and a nod of his head.

'Morning Sergeant, anything to report?'

Bellows passed him the sheet of A4, informing them of the accident and the man who was in custody.

At that moment Detective Inspector Robert Laxton came through the door.

'Ahh Robert!' exclaimed Wilberton, lifting his eyes from the report.

'Read that,' he said, handing him the report.

Laxton had a deep frown on his forehead as he took in the details of the accident that had occurred on the stretch of the A1 that ran through Lincoln.

'Have the relatives of the deceased and injured been informed?' he muttered.

'We have ascertained that Mr and Mrs Malling have an only daughter and a brother Brian Malling,' said Bellows.

'Have we got the address of the brother?' enquired Laxton.

Bellows nodded his head and pushed a register along the counter to him. Laxton ran his eyes over the few names on the almost empty page.

'Brian Malling, 34 Rochester Lane, Holton-le-Clay,' he mumbled almost inaudibly. 'I'll get down there after I've had a coffee.'

'Billings!' shouted Bellows.

'Yes Sergeant,' a cheerful voice called out.

'Two coffees,' snapped the sergeant.

'Coming up Sarge.'

Laxton smiled at the cocky reply as he followed the chief into his office.

A few minutes later the young constable came in with the drinks and placed them on the desk. Laxton picked one up and tentatively took a sip of the hot drink.

'First of all we'll check to make sure that he is in,' announced the chief as he reached out for the phone.

'Hello is that Brian Malling?' There was long pause, before he went on, 'Have you been informed of the tragic accident on Saturday morning?'

There was another pause as he listened to the brief reply; nodding his head at the phone.

'You have. Yes I'm sure it has been a great shock to you,' he said in a voice full of feeling before going on to ask him what would be a convenient time for one of his officers to visit.

'About ten o'clock this morning, I reckon that will be okay.'

He put the phone down and turned his attention to Laxton, who was just finishing his coffee. He lifted his arm and checked his wrist watch. It showed nine a.m.

'You've got one hour to get there before he goes out Robert,' he told him.

The inspector pushed the chair back and got to his feet.

'I'd better be off then,' he announced.

A few minutes later he was climbing in his car. After negotiating the busy centre of Lincoln he turned on to the road that would take him to Louth. There was a look of satisfaction on his face as he passed through the town and saw a sign indicating Holton-le-Clay on the Grimsby road. Twenty minutes later he turned off the main highway and made the short journey to the pleasant village of Holton-le-Clay. He was suitably impressed by the well-tended properties in the village. Eventually he came to Rochester Lane; dropping down into second gear he drove slowly along the lane as he checked the properties until he finally came to number thirty-six.

The large, imposing house stood well back from the lane. There was a lawn either side of a cobbled drive that led to a garage. A row of conifers ran along the front of the property.

Quite impressive, thought Laxton as he drew onto the drive and climbed out of the car.

He reached up and gave a couple of sharp raps on the large brass lion that hung on the oak door. There was a sound of footsteps and the door opened.

'Mr Brian Malling?' enquired Laxton of the short

fat man in front of him.

The man nodded his head and smiled, his round face lighting up as he stood back.

'Please come in Inspector, I've been expecting you!' he exclaimed.

Laxton nodded his thanks, strode over the threshold and followed him into a large lounge. Malling indicated an easy chair. Laxton sat down and shuffled his backside as he made himself comfortable.

'Would you like a drink?' enquired the stocky man.

The inspector raised a hand and shook his head. Malling took a seat opposite him.

'Now then Inspector, how can I help you?'

'First of all let me say how sorry I am at the death of your brother and his wife,' said Laxton softly.

'Yes it is quite a blow,' Malling replied, running his hand over his balding head.

'Are you and his daughter the only relatives?' the inspector put to him.

Brian nodded his head, telling him, 'His daughter, Rebecca, is at university in London.'

'Has she been informed?' enquired Laxton.

'She rang me on Saturday afternoon,' replied Malling, nodding his head, before going on to tell him: 'She was informed by the police, a few hours after the accident. I'm afraid she took it badly.'

'Can you give me her address and telephone number?'

The stocky heavily built man struggled to his feet and went over to a sideboard and pulled open a drawer; taking out a slip of paper, he wrote the address of her home in Langworth where she was staying and her phone number on it, he handed the slip of paper to the inspector.

After a quick glance at it, Laxton pushed it in his pocket and got to his feet.

'Sorry I've had to bother you Mister Malling,' he intoned as he turned to leave.

'No problem,' rejoined Malling as the inspector opened the door and left.

Laxton checked his watch as he fastened his seatbelt, it was ten minutes past twelve; he was feeling hungry. He cast his mind back to when he had been in the area; he recalled a pub named the 'Red Lion' where he'd had a decent meal. It was situated about two miles further along the main road. Five minutes after leaving Malling's property he pulled into the car park at the front of the pub in question. The sound of soft music met him as he pushed open the heavy door and walked up to the bar. A tall slim man was wiping the top of the bar down. Drying his hands on the towel, he approached Laxton.

'Now then sir what can I do for you?' he enquired, a friendly smile on his face.

'I'll have a pint of bitter shandy please,' requested the inspector as he ran his eyes down the menu list that was on a board standing on the bar.

The barman handed him the glass of bitter shandy. 'That will be one pound fifty sir,' he said.

Laxton paid for the drink, picked up the frothy pint and took a long drink. 'Ahh,' he grunted, a smile of pleasure on his face as he placed the glass on the bar.

'Will there be anything else?' enquired the barman.

'Yes!' exclaimed the inspector, nodding his head at the menu. 'I'll have one of the meals advertised on your board.'

'Which one would you like?'

'I'll have the scampi and chips,' Laxton told him.

'That will be three pounds fifty,' announced the barman, before pointing with his forefinger. 'Take a seat at one of the tables, the waitress will bring it to you.'

Laxton nodded his thanks before placing the money on the counter and walking over to one of the tables that the barman had indicated, where he sat down just as the barman went over to a hatch at the back of the bar and called out in a loud voice, 'One scampi and chips Mavis!'

The jukebox was playing a rendition of Frank Sinatra singing 'Strangers in the Night'.

Laxton ran his eyes round the large room as the haunting music filled the air. A large print of *The Haywain* hung on the wall, a small lamp above it made it almost come to life.

Reaching out, he picked up his pint. He was just in the act of taking a drink when a woman with long blonde hair approached the table carrying a tray.

'There you are sir,' she trilled as she leaned over and placed it on the table in front of him, giving him a view of her deep cleavage before handing him a knife and fork, then she turned and walked away, her high heels making a clipping sound on the tiled floor.

Laxton picked up the knife and fork; he paused for few seconds as he eyed the plate full of battered scampi and chips, before tucking in. A few minutes later he leaned back and patted his stomach. He'd really enjoyed that, he told himself, as he picked up his glass and finished off his drink. The dining area was filling up as he got to his feet and made his way to the exit.

'Thank you sir,' a voice called out. He raised his arm in acknowledgement as he pushed open the door and stepped outside and walked across the car park and climbed into his car.

'Now let me see,' he muttered as he tried to place Langworth.

Suddenly it came to him.

'I remember now, it's just a few miles outside Lincoln,' he muttered to himself as he accelerated out on to the main road.

It was two o'clock when Rebecca arrived back at her home in Langworth. She had just put the kettle on when the front doorbell rang.

'Now who could this be?' she muttered as she went to answer it. She opened the door. A tall man stood in front of her.

'Miss Rebecca Malling?' he enquired, a smile on his ruggedly handsome face.

'Yes,' she replied, nodding her head.

'I'm Detective Inspector Laxton of the Lincoln Police, would it be possible for me to have a word with you?'

'Won't you come in?' the young woman told him, standing back and opening the door wide.

Laxton stepped into the hallway with a 'Thank you,' and followed her into the comfortable, spacious lounge.

'I'm just about to make a cup of tea, would you like one?' she asked him after indicating for him to take a seat.

'That would be ideal,' he replied as he made himself comfortable in the seat of one of the two easy chairs.

A few minutes later she came into the lounge carrying a tray with two cups of tea and a plate full of biscuits on it.

'Now then Inspector what can I do for you?' she enquired as she took a seat in the other easy chair opposite him.

Laxton took a tentative sip of his hot cup of tea before telling her that he was making enquiries regarding the car accident that had killed her father and badly injured her mother.

'I'm afraid my mum is also dead,' she told him huskily.

'Oh I am sorry to hear that,' he muttered as he placed his cup on the tray. 'When did that happen?'

'Yesterday morning,' she informed him. 'She passed away in front of me.'

The inspector shook his head slowly from side to side. 'That must have been an upsetting experience for you,' he told her feelingly.

She just glanced down at her clasped hands in her lap, a little overcome. Laxton reached out and patted her arm.

'Never mind my dear. These happenings do come to try us,' he said in an effort to console her.

'What was it you wanted to see me about Inspector?' she asked him.

Laxton picked up his cup of tea and took another drink before telling her that he was investigating the accident to check where to apportion blame.

'From all the information we have it seems as though the van driver was at fault,' he informed her, before asking her if she had anything to add.

'Not really,' she mumbled, her mouth full of biscuit. 'I would like to ask you if you could enlighten me regarding the law of adoption.'

'In what way do you mean?' he put to her.

She went on to tell him of the predicament that she was in and of the letter in the box showing the payment of five amounts of two thousand pounds. Going over to the drawer she took out the metal box, opened it and handed the envelope to the inspector.

Taking it from her he studied the words 'Adoption payments' written on the front of the envelope for a few seconds, before taking out the folded sheet of paper and opening it out.

'Mmm,' he muttered as he ran his eyes over the figures written on it. 'What is the significance of these payments?'

'I haven't a clue,' confessed Rebecca with a shrug of her shoulders.

Laxton turned to her and asked her, 'Can I take this with me?'

She nodded her head. 'Yes I don't see why not,' she told him.

Thanking her, the inspector folded the letter, put it back inside the envelope and placed it in his inside pocket before leaning forward, his fingers interlocked. There was a thoughtful expression on his face as he addressed her.

'Now let me see,' he began. 'You say that you are twenty years old. It is now 1984. That means that you were born in 1964.'

He paused for a moment as he studied the situation, something in the back of his mind was niggling him. He shook his head in annoyance.

'I'll check on it when I get back to the station,' he assured her as he got to his feet in readiness to leave.

'I hope you will inform me if you come up with anything to do with my adoption Inspector,' she asked him as he walked to the door.

Thanking the young woman for the hospitality and assuring her that he would get back to her, he left the bungalow, climbed into his car and drove off.

Chapter 4

Laxton was deep in thought as he wended his way through the open countryside; his brain was working overtime as he joined the busy main road to Lincoln.

On arrival at headquarters some twenty minutes later he entered the outer office.

Sergeant Bellows was getting a bit of an ear bashing from an elderly lady as he went up to the counter.

'Excuse me my dear,' he said, addressing the somewhat harassed old lady before turning to Bellows and asking him, 'is the chief busy?'

The red-faced sergeant turned away from the little woman and told the inspector, 'No, there's no one with him at the moment.'

Laxton nodded his head in acknowledgement at the sergeant, before walking across the room and opening the chief's door.

'Ahh Robert!' exclaimed Wilberton, looking up at the inspector as he came through the door. 'I've just been informed that the woman who was involved in the accident has died.'

Laxton had a grim expression on his face as he pulled up a chair and sat opposite the chief; after making himself comfortable he told him, 'Yes chief, I've just interviewed the woman's daughter Rebecca; she told me of the tragic loss of her mother and father.'

'Mmm, it seems that the driver of the van that was involved in the accident has plenty of explaining to do,' Wilberton retorted, his brow deeply furrowed.

'There is something else that I would like to look into,' confided Laxton, leaning forward in his chair, his hands clasped in front of him.

'And what would that be?' enquired the chief.

Laxton looked down at his well-polished shoes for a few seconds before going on to tell Wilberton of the problem that Rebecca Malling had told him about, regarding her birth certificate and adoption papers.

'What was wrong with them?' asked the chief, dipping his head and looking at Laxton over the rim of his glasses.

The inspector gave a shrug of his shoulders explaining, 'There aren't any.'

'There aren't any?' repeated the chief questioningly.

'That is what she's been told by the department of birth and deaths,' explained Laxton as he reached into his inside pocket and drew out the envelope that he had received from Rebecca Malling and placed it on the desk in front of Wilberton.

'What's this?' enquired the chief, reaching out and picking up the envelope.

'It was among the belongings of the girl's deceased

parents,' explained Laxton.

Wilberton, a deep frown forming on his forehead, as he read the instructions on the front of the envelope stating that the documents should be destroyed. Taking out the folded sheet of paper, he opened it out and ran his eyes over it for a couple of minutes before reading out loud, 'Five payments of two thousand pounds for the adoption of one girl.' It was signed R Malling.

He turned the sheet of paper over to check whether there was anything else written on it.

'This isn't much to go on,' he stated, shaking his head.

Laxton leaned forward in his chair and addressed the chief.

'Rebecca Malling has been in touch with the Office of Births and Deaths in Boston and has been told that there is no record of a child being born to a Ronald and Marion Malling in the year when their daughter Rebecca was supposed to have been born.'

Wilberton, deep in thought, beat a tattoo on the desk with his knuckles as he studied the seriousness of the situation.

'There is something very fishy about this Robert,' he muttered, suddenly straightening up in his chair and looking the inspector in the eyes. 'I want you to drop everything else that you may be involved in and concentrate on discovering the facts surrounding the birth of this young woman,' he declared sharply.

Laxton nodded his head in agreement as he got to his feet.

'I'll get down to Boston and have a word with the appropriate department,' he said firmly as he turned and made for the door.

A few minutes later he climbed into his car and drove out of the station car park.

The sun was shining from a predominantly blue sky, although heavy clouds were beginning to show on the horizon as he joined the busy A46. Forty minutes later he was pulling into the car park of the Births and Deaths Department in Boston; easing his body out of the car he approached the door marked 'Entrance'. Pushing his way through the glass door, he went over to a long counter. A young woman who had been sat at a desk came over to him.

'Can I help you sir?' the blonde petite young woman enquired politely.

He explained to her who he was before telling her that he was enquiring after certain information regarding birth certification. On discovering that he was with the police she invited him into the main office. After listening carefully she asked the inspector to bear with her for a moment while she went to the person in charge. A few seconds later a heavily built bespectacled man who looked to be in his forties approached him.

'Now then sir, I'm John Griffiths the manager, how can I help you?' he enquired pleasantly.

'I'm Inspector Laxton and I'm looking into the birth details of a young lady named Rebecca Malling,' he explained.

Griffiths plucked at his bottom lip for a couple of seconds as he mulled over what the inspector had told him.

'Rebecca Malling you say?'

He paused for a moment and ran his hand over his balding head before informing the inspector that a woman of that name had been to see him earlier.

'I was going to get in touch with the powers that be to see if they could resolve the problem of her identity,' he declared.

'Can I see the records?' asked Laxton.

'Yes, of course you can,' replied Griffiths, going over to a large metal cabinet and opening one of its wide drawers.

He reached into the drawer and lifted out a pile of documents.

'There you are,' he said, handing them to the inspector. 'Look through those.'

Laxton thanked him and took the documents over to a table, pulled up a chair and sat down. Reaching into his inside pocket he took out a case which contained his glasses, taking them out he put them on and proceeded to check through the long list of names. After a few minutes he straightened up, a deep frown on his forehead. He had drawn a blank. Taking off his glasses he turned to Griffiths who was sat at his desk.

'There doesn't seem to be any reference whatsoever to a Mr and Mrs Malling having registered a birth,' he told him.

'No and there aren't any records of it anywhere else in the country,' stated the manager adding, 'I've gone into it thoroughly.'

Laxton got to his feet and walked across the office stroking his chin. He was deep in thought as he approached Griffiths.

'Is there any way that we can discover some sort of

evidence to trace the people involved in the adoption of Rebecca Malling?' he put to him as he placed his glasses in the case and put them back in his pocket.

Griffiths shook his head negatively. 'I'm afraid I can't help you inspector.'

Laxton thanked him and his assistant for their co-operation before taking his leave. A few minutes later he climbed into his car and exited the car park. After he had made his way through the busy centre of Boston, he settled down to a steady and somewhat pleasant drive through the open Lincolnshire countryside, his destination Lincoln police headquarters. An hour or so later he drove into the headquarters car park. Jumping out of the car, he opened the glass door and entered the reception area.

'Just in time,' declared a smiling Bellows. 'We've just put the kettle on.'

Laxton returned the smile and nodded his appreciation as he walked across the room to the chief's office and knocked on the door.

'I'll send you a coffee in,' the sergeant called as he opened the door and went in.

'Now then Robert, what have you come up with?' enquired the chief as the inspector shut the door behind him.

Laxton, a serious expression on his face, took a seat before going through everything that he had gleaned from his visit to the Births and Deaths department in Boston regarding the birth of Rebecca Malling.

'Mmm,' muttered Wilberton, a deep frown on his forehead as he went over in his mind what he had been told. 'This leaves us with a problem.'

He leaned forward, placed his elbows on the desk

and clasped his hands as he studied the situation. After a few seconds he addressed the inspector. 'Have you any ideas as to how we can solve it?' he put to him.

Laxton, his arms folded and his eyes half closed, was silent as he went through facts so far before making a suggestion. 'I think it would be a good idea to search through the records and check if there are any cases of children going missing around the same time as Rebecca Malling, specifically around nineteen sixty-eight.'

'I tend to agree with you!' exclaimed Wilberton, reaching out and picking up the phone.

'We'll get on to records right away,' he added as he dialled a number.

At that moment Bellows came in carrying a tray with two mugs of coffee on it. Laxton and the chief smiled their thanks as he placed them on the desk and withdrew.

'Is that records?' asked the chief, as Bellows closed the door behind him. 'Ahh, good!' he exclaimed. 'Will it be possible for you to dig up some information regarding any abductions in the UK, of children reported during the period from around nineteen sixty-five to nineteen seventy?' he enquired.

Reaching out he picked up a mug of coffee and took a sip while he waited for an answer to his request. After what seemed a long five minutes he received a reply.

Picking up a pen, he proceeded to write a lengthy passage on a note pad. When he had finished he thanked the person on the other end of the phone before placing the receiver back on its cradle and turning his attention to the inspector.

'According to the information I've received. There

were seven children reported missing during the period that I indicated.' He paused for a moment to take another drink of his coffee before going on. 'It seems that three of them were eventually found.'

He paused again and looked Laxton in the eyes, a solemn expression on his face as he lowered his voice and told him, 'The other four are still undetected.'

Laxton lifted his mug and drank the rest of his coffee before checking his watch. It was four o'clock.

'I'll get down to records and look up the names of the four that are still missing,' he told the chief. 'I'll interview the parents tomorrow.'

Wilberton nodded his head in agreement as the inspector got to his feet and turned to go through the door. A few minutes later he had manoeuvred his car out of the station car park and was making his way to the records office in the centre of Lincoln. On arrival he entered the main building. Two glass doors confronted him; on one of them was written 'Records'. Opening it he approached a gaunt looking man sat at a desk; he was poring over a document, he looked up through what looked like two jam jar bottoms as the tall detective approached him, his creased face broke into a half smile.

'My name is Lander, er, Arthur Lander. Can I help you?' he asked, taking off the thick rimmed glasses.

Laxton identified himself before explaining to him that he wanted some information regarding missing children.

'Oh yes,' Lander replied, adding, 'Chief Inspector Wilberton has been enquiring earlier about them. I put them in here.'

He bent down and opened the bottom drawer of

his desk. Laxton clasped his hands in front of him; he gazed down at the top of the man's balding head as he waited patiently for him to find the documents. After a few minutes of 'tut tutting' under his breath as he shuffled through a thick heap of papers, he finally found what he was looking for.

'Ahh,' he muttered. 'Here we are.'

Straightening up he placed what looked like four or five sheets of paper on the desk.

'There you are sir!' he exclaimed, as he handed the documents to the inspector. 'If you would like to study them now you can take them over there,' he told him, pointing to another desk on the other side of the large office.

Laxton thanked him and made his way to the desk that the man had indicated; pulling a chair from under it, he sat down and placed the papers on the desk in front of him. There was a deep frown on his forehead as he went through the harrowing details of the children that had gone missing around sixteen years ago. According to their ages they were all abducted within a six month period. Their names were:

Margaret Bennings, who was aged three and a half when she went missing. Elizabeth Jayne Watling, aged four. Caroline Gateland, aged four, and James Batley aged three and a half. Laxton took out a note book and wrote down the four names and last known addresses of the parents. After stretching his arms out wide to ease his aching back, he got to his feet and went over to Lander, thanking him for his help and returning the sheets of paper.

'I reckon the information that I've gleaned from these documents will prove very useful,' he told him as he put his note book back in his inside pocket.

Lander got to his feet as the inspector prepared to leave.

'I'm pleased to have been of some assistance,' he called after Laxton as the tall detective strode towards the exit.

The inspector checked his watch as he climbed into his car. It was four forty-five.

He was deep in thought as he made his way back to Old Bolingbroke.

'Your dinner's in the oven,' Annie informed him on his arrival back home.

He smiled his thanks as she jumped on her bike and pedalled off.

Horatio was milling around his feet as he walked across the driveway. The cat gave a squeal as Laxton accidentally trod on his paw.

'Get out of the way Horatio,' he snapped a little testily as he stepped through the door and made his way to the kitchen. Taking his dinner out of the oven, he sat down and enjoyed it. After a shower he settled down for the evening.

Chapter 5

Laxton was deep in thought as he climbed into his car and drove out of Old Bolingbroke and set off on his journey to Dunham, a small village situated near the River Trent some twenty miles from Lincoln along the A57. He smiled to himself as he recalled the times when he used to compete in fishing matches at Dunham Bridge in his teens. He gave a deep sigh and shook his head. 'That was a long time ago,' he muttered to himself as he changed down a gear to negotiate a sharp bend in the road. After half an hour's drive along the busy road had gone by, he approached Dunham Bridge which was a toll bridge; showing his credentials to the official at the toll gate, he was waved through. Ten minutes later he turned off the main highway and wended his way through the village streets and lanes until he came to what he was looking for; the aptly named 'Water Lane'. Dropping down into second gear, he made his way slowly along the lane. He gave a nod of satisfaction as he drew up outside the property that he was searching for – number sixteen. Climbing out of the car he opened the rickety gate and walked up the path that divided the small front garden of the whitewashed cottage that was in the middle of a row of six. He lifted the iron doorknocker on the wooden door and gave a sharp 'rat-a-tat'.

A dog could be heard barking incessantly from inside the cottage as the sound of footsteps approaching the door could be heard.

'Shut up Rocky,' a man's gruff voice snapped.

The dog's bark was reduced to a low growl; there was a creaking noise as the door opened to reveal the harassed figure of a thickset, whiskery man in his fifties. He was busy tucking his shirt into his trousers.

'Sorry about the delay,' he muttered. 'I was on the toilet when I heard the knock on the door.'

'Mr Benning?' enquired the inspector.

Benning nodded his head, a questioning look in his eyes as he took in the tall figure standing in front of him.

'Yes, what can I do for you?' he enquired a little sharply.

Laxton identified himself.

'The police?' snapped Benning a look of incredulity on his face. 'I've done nothing wrong.'

The inspector raised his right hand and smiled. 'I'm not here for you,' he assured him. 'I'm making enquiries about the abduction of a young girl named Margaret Benning.'

'Our Margaret!' the short man exclaimed. 'What about her. Have you found her?'

Laxton gave a faint smile as he shook his head.

'It's nothing like that I'm afraid,' he replied before

informing him, 'I'm just making enquiries about her.'

'Just a minute I'll call the wife,' said a puzzled Benning as he stepped back from the door and called out at the top of his voice, 'Joan!'

A woman's voice from the rear of the cottage shouted. 'What do you want?'

'There's someone at the door asking about out Margaret.'

A few seconds later a short bonny woman who looked to be in her early forties, her long dark hair tied in a bun at the back of her head, came to the door. She looked up at the inspector who introduced himself.

Joan Benning gave a quick glance up and down the lane.

'You'd better come inside Inspector,' she told him in a low voice.

Laxton ducked his head under the low door frame and followed her into a small lounge comfortably furnished with a well-worn three piece suite and a polished top table. A large oil painting of a country scene hung over a stone fireplace. In the corner was a cage containing a budgie which was jumping up and down chirping away.

'Shut up Basil,' snapped Bill, giving a sharp tap on the cage with his forefinger, as he took a seat beside his wife on the settee opposite Laxton who had settled himself down on one of the easy chairs.

'Now then Inspector, what is it that you want know?' she asked sharply as she pushed a frond of slightly greying hair back from over her blue eyes.

Laxton, a friendly smile on his face, addressed the woman.

'I'm making enquiries about your daughter who went missing around sixteen years ago,' he told her.

The woman put her hand to her mouth, her eyes wide with shock.

'Have you found her?' she enquired in a strained voice.

'That's what I'm here to find out,' explained the inspector. 'Would it be possible for you to give me a few details regarding the disappearance of your daughter?'

Joan Benning turned to her husband, who was standing behind her listening intently to what was being said.

'As I recall, we were shopping in the supermarket weren't we Bill?' she stated.

Her husband nodded his head in agreement before she went on to tell the inspector, 'We only had Margaret at that time.'

She paused again and plucked at her bottom lip; she had a deep frown on her forehead as she cast her mind back.

'As I was saying, we had taken her with us to the supermarket. Margaret, she was only three and a half at the time, was with me.'

At that moment a cool breeze wafted through the bungalow as the front door swung open followed by a bang as it was shut.

Joan stopped talking for a moment and shook her head in annoyance.

'That will be our Ronnie,' she muttered as a young man who looked to be about sixteen walked through the door. He stood for a couple of seconds and looked at

Laxton before turning his attention to his parents.

'What's going on Mum?' he asked, a questioning look on his freckled face.

'Never you mind our Ronald. It's none of your business,' replied his dad, a little sharply, telling him, 'Either sit down and be quiet or go into the kitchen.'

Young Ronnie thought over what his dad had told him then with a shrug of his shoulders, he turned and walked out of the room.

'Now where was I?' said Joan as she reached up and pushed a few strands of hair back that had fallen over her eyes.

'You were in the supermarket,' the inspector reminded her.

'Oh yes!' she exclaimed, before explaining: 'I turned to Bill to discuss the prices of some of the goods on display, when I noticed that our Margaret wasn't with us.'

She paused for a few seconds as she cast her mind back to that fateful moment, tears forming in her eyes. Bill put his arm around her shoulder comfortingly as she took out a tissue that had been tucked in her sleeve and dabbed her eyes. He turned his attention to the inspector.

'We searched all over the supermarket, but we couldn't find her,' he explained, shaking his head slowly from side to side, adding in a low voice: 'It seemed impossible that she could have disappeared in so short a time.'

Laxton stroked his chin as he mulled over what he had been told before trying another line of approach. 'Did your daughter have any distinguishing marks on her body?' he enquired.

'No,' the couple replied in unison, shaking their heads negatively.

'There is just one thing more,' he stated as he got to his feet to leave. 'I would like you to take a blood test.'

'Does this mean that you have found our Margaret?' asked Joan.

The inspector looked into her eyes and smiled before telling her, 'I'm afraid I can't reassure you on that point, Mrs Benning, at the moment I am just making enquiries.'

'What about the blood test?' asked Bill as the inspector reached out to open the door, he stopped and turned to the couple,

'When you've had the test I want you to instruct the hospital to send the results to the Lincoln police station for examination,' he replied, adding somewhat secretively, 'we will eventually get in touch with you.'

Closing the door behind him Laxton walked up the garden path; large spots of rain were beginning to fall from a darkening sky as he climbed in his car.

The inspector had a thoughtful expression on his face as he drove along the lane and out on to the main road that led back to Lincoln. The windscreen wipers were swishing from side to side as they fought to clear the heavy rain that lashed against them as he joined the heavy traffic. Half an hour or so later he arrived back at police headquarters; pulling into the car park he disembarked and swiftly made his way into the building.

'Is the chief available?' he asked Bellows as he entered the front office.

The sergeant nodded his head, telling him, 'I'll

send you a coffee in.'

Laxton thanked him before knocking on the chief's door and walking in to the sound of Bellows loud voice shouting, 'Billings!'

Chief Inspector Wilberton, who had been looking through a couple of documents, greeted him with a nod of his head as he entered and indicated for him to take a seat. Putting the documents to one side he addressed Laxton after he had settled down.

'What have you got then Robert?' he enquired, dipping his head and looking at him over the rim of his glasses.

The inspector went through the details of his meeting with Rebecca Malling. This was followed by an in-depth account of his subsequent investigation of another of the families in question, the Bennings.

Wilberton interlocked his fingers in his lap as he leaned back in his chair, his brow creased as he thought through the details of what Laxton had told him. After a few seconds he came to a decision.

'Robert!' he exclaimed. 'I've come to the conclusion that we should keep what we learn about the people involved in the, what looks like, abductions, to ourselves for the time being.'

At that moment PC Billings knocked on the door and came in carrying a tray with two mugs of coffee on it and placed it on the desk in front of the chief.

Wilberton, a look of irritation on his face at being stopped when he was in full flow, nodded his thanks, before going on. 'As I was saying, we'll keep our conclusions to ourselves until we know for sure who the parents are.'

Laxton reached out and picked up one of the mugs

of steaming coffee and took a sip before replying. 'I reckon you are right Chief,' he mumbled as he wiped his lips with the back of his hand. 'Until we've discovered who the children's natural parents are, I agree we should keep it to ourselves.'

He paused for a moment as he took another drink of his coffee, then went on.

'After we've checked out all the sets of parents whose children have mysteriously disappeared, it may be possible to come to some conclusion as to who may be responsible.'

Wilberton was silent for a few seconds as he went carefully through in his mind, what Laxton had told him.

'Robert, considering that we have a lead regarding Rebecca Malling, I think the best way forward is to concentrate on the three girls that have gone missing; you can go into the case of the young boy at a later date,' he expounded.

The inspector nodded his head in agreement before stating that he would interview Jean Gateland next at her address which was 33 Moreton Drive, Grimsby. He pulled his jacket sleeve back and checked his watch – it showed twelve thirty.

'I'll get down there right away,' he told the chief as he got to his feet and strode purposefully out of the office.

It was still raining heavily as he made a quick dash to his car; climbing in, he started the engine and drove out of the car park.

'It will soon be time for me to think about getting something to eat,' he muttered to himself; he was beginning to feel hungry.

Ten minutes later he had cleared the busy city centre and was on his way to Grimsby. The rain was still coming down heavily when he eventually entered the busy centre of the town. The wipers were swishing from side to side as he peered through the misted windscreen.

'If I remember correctly, Moreton Drive is off Cleethorpes Road,' he muttered to himself as he drove slowly through the busy traffic keeping his eyes peeled.

Eventually he saw the road sign – Cleethorpes Road. Turning onto it he kept his eyes open for Moreton Drive. He gave grunt of satisfaction as he came to it. A couple of minutes later he drew up outside number thirty-three. The rain was beginning to abate a little as he banged the car door shut behind him; opening a wooden gate he walked up to the glass panelled door and rang the bell. He stood clasping his hands in front of him as he waited patiently for someone to answer it; after a few seconds the sound of high heels could be heard approaching the door.

The door opened to reveal a tall, slim, smartly dressed woman in her late forties.

'Mrs Gateland?' asked the inspector politely.

'Yes. Can I help you?' she enquired smilingly.

The inspector introduced himself before telling her that he was investigating the disappearance of her daughter Caroline in 1968.

'Won't you come in?' asked Mrs Gateland, standing to one side.

'Thank you,' said Laxton, with a nod of his head, as he stepped into the hallway and followed the woman into a large well equipped kitchen. A heavily built man was reclining in a wicker armchair reading a newspaper as they entered; he looked up at Laxton over the rim of his glasses.

'Oh er, hello,' he said falteringly as he got to his feet.

'This is my husband Michael,' she explained, adding, 'Michael this is Inspector Laxton.'

The man took off his glasses, stepped forward and shook hands with the inspector.

'Have a seat,' he said, pointing to a chair. Laxton thanked him and sat down.

'The inspector is making enquiries about our Caroline going missing,' Jean Gateland told her husband.

Michael Gateland stood for a few seconds stroking his chin; he was deep in thought. He looked at Laxton, his brow creased questioningly. 'Didn't the police get enough information during the time they were investigating our daughter's disappearance in 1968?' he queried.

The inspector leaned forward in his chair and clasped his hands in front of him as he thought over his reply before turning to Gateland.

'Yes I reckon they did but investigations at that time came to nothing. Certain facts have come to our notice recently that may help in finding your daughter,' he told him a little guardedly.

Jean Gateland's hand went to her mouth; she had a shocked expression on her face.

'Are you saying that you know where she is?' she said, almost inaudibly.

'No I'm not saying that,' he told her firmly with a shake of his head. 'All I'm saying is that we may have a lead. It all depends on the circumstances.'

At that moment the door burst open and a pretty blonde girl in her teens came in.

'Hi Mum, hi Dad,' she carolled as she leaned over and gave her mum a kiss on the cheek, this was followed by her going over to her dad and kissing him on the top of his balding head.

'This is our daughter Marina,' announced Michael, reaching up and running his fingers through his thinning hair.

'What's going on Mum?' asked the fourteen-year-old Marina, eyeing the inspector as she pushed back a wayward lock of her hair that had fallen over her blue eyes.

'This is Inspector Laxton,' her mum told her.

Laxton nodded his head at the girl, a friendly smile on his rugged face.

'He's here asking questions regarding our Caroline's disappearance.'

'Marina wasn't born when her sister went missing,' she explained to the inspector.

'What did you mean by circumstances, Inspector?' enquired her husband, getting back to the subject in hand.

'Well, first of all I will require both of you to have a blood test,' he stated, looking from one to the other. He paused for a moment before adding, 'then we can take it from there.'

'Does this mean we might be seeing our daughter again?' asked Jean Gateland.

'As I've already told you, it all depends on the circumstances,' replied Laxton as he got to his feet to leave.

'What about the blood sample Inspector?' Michael Gateland called after him as he was making his way to the front door. Laxton turned and looked at him, questioningly.

'What do we do with it?'

'Inform the hospital to send it to forensics at Lincoln police headquarters,' the inspector told him before opening the door and walking out.

There were just a few spots of rain coming down as Laxton made his way along the garden path on his way to his car. He glanced up at the sky; a patch of blue was showing amid the heavy clouds that were being swept along by the strong wind. He climbed into his car and sat for a few seconds as he checked his notes for the address of the next family that he was to visit: Mr and Mrs Watling.

Their address was 6 Church Lane, Swallow, near Market Rasen. His brow furrowed for a moment as he cast his mind back to when he had last visited the village of Swallow; as far as he could remember, it was nestled in the countryside just off the main road between Louth and Market Rasen. He checked his watch as he fastened his seatbelt; it showed one forty-five. He figured that the journey would take him around an hour, this would give him plenty of time to stop on the way and have a quick meal before completing his investigations.

The rain had stopped and heavy clouds were making way for the sun which was just beginning to show as he put his foot down and accelerated away. Ten minutes later he pulled into the car park of an impressive olde worlde pub, its thatched roof giving it a medieval look; signs outside the pub advertised appetising meals.

'This should be just the job,' he muttered to himself as he climbed out of the car and strode to the pub door. Opening it he approached the bar. A buxom, blonde-haired, well-endowed woman greeted him.

'Yes sir, what would you like?' she enquired, a broad smile on her face.

Laxton ran his eyes over the sign at the back of the bar which advertised the various meals on offer. After a slight pause to make up his mind, he told her, 'I'll have the haddock and chips please and a pint of bitter shandy.'

After writing the order down, she poured the drink and passed it to him, telling him, 'That will be five pounds fifty sir.'

He was then told to take a seat at one of the tables. After what seemed an interminably long time, a young waitress arrived carrying a tray with his meal on it. Thanking her he tucked in to the appetising meal. Twenty minutes later he leaned back in his seat, a satisfied expression on his face.

Finishing his drink he got to his feet and made his way out of the pub, climbed into his car and continued his journey.

Half an hour later he negotiated the roundabout on the outskirts of Louth and took the A631 to Market Rasen. Six miles further on he came to a sign pointing to Swallow. Turning off the main road he made his way along the country lane that led to the quiet olde worlde village. Ten minutes or so later he came upon Church Lane; turning down it he drove slowly until he came to a group of semi-detached cottages opposite a beautiful church. Stopping the car outside number six, he climbed out, opened the gate and strode along the path which was lined with daffodils, to the front door. Reaching out he pressed the bell. He could just make out a woman's figure through the small stained glass window, approaching the door; a few seconds later the door opened to reveal a slim, attractive woman with long light brown hair. She looked to be in her forties. *Quite a good looking lady*, thought Laxton.

'Mrs Marjory Watling?' he enquired.

'Yes, can I help you?' she said in a friendly tone of voice as she looked up at the tall detective.

The inspector identified himself before going on to tell her that he was investigating the disappearance of her daughter Elizabeth.

'Won't you come in?' she instructed him.

'Thank you,' replied Laxton, a friendly smile on his face as he stepped into the hallway.

Marjory Watling closed the door before leading him along the hallway and into a spacious, pleasantly warm conservatory; she pointed to a comfortable looking wicker chair.

'Would you like a coffee?' she asked him as he sat down on the thickly cushioned chair.

'Thank you, that would be nice,' he told her, nodding his head in appreciation.

She returned his smile before turning to go back along the hallway.

Laxton sat back and relaxed. He cast his eyes around the all glass conservatory; the windows were covered by slatted blinds which were open, letting in the sun. A photograph of a man in his thirties stood on a small cabinet in the corner. Exotic potted plants lined the low walls. Bamboo pipes hanging over the doorway played a tune as they swayed in the light breeze that came through the outer door. He half closed his eyes and breathed in the aromatic scent from the plants.

A few minutes later Marjory Watling came in carrying a tray with two mugs of coffee and a plate of assorted biscuits on it. Placing the tray on a small round table in front of him, she took a seat on the opposite side of the table and addressed him. 'Now then Inspector!' she exclaimed as she reached out for a biscuit. 'What was it you were about to ask me regarding my daughter Elizabeth?'

Laxton took a sip of his coffee before explaining to her that certain circumstances had recently arisen which could throw some light on the little girl's disappearance.

She was just about to pop the rest of the biscuit into her mouth when she suddenly stopped.

'Are you telling me that it might be possible for me to get my daughter back?' she enquired, forcefully.

Laxton gave a shake of his head as he reached out for a biscuit.

'I wouldn't go as far as to say that Mrs Watling,' he replied a little evasively. He took a bite of the biscuit before going on to tell her that he wanted a few facts from her.

'What is it you want to know?' she asked.

'Well first of all, did she have any marks or scars on her body?'

She pursed her lips, her blue eyes half closed as she cast her mind back.

'The only thing that I can recall is that when she was two years old she was playing on the mat in the kitchen.' She paused for a moment, her hand on her forehead, before going on. 'I had climbed on a chair to reach the top cupboard that was over the worktop. When I stepped down I put my foot on her hand; I was wearing high heeled shoes at the time – she screamed out in pain.'

She had a faraway look in her eyes as she reached out for her cup of coffee and took a drink.

'Was she injured?' enquired Laxton.

She gave a nod of her head, telling him that her daughter was badly hurt.

She stopped again and finished off her coffee before continuing.

'The doctor examined her and informed us that she had broken a bone in her hand and that the middle finger would most likely be deformed.'

The inspector, who had been taking notes, placed the pen and the book in his pocket before enquiring, 'Would it be possible to have a word with your husband before I leave?'

'I'm afraid that won't be possible,' she told him, a sad expression on her face as she added, 'George died of bowel cancer five years ago.'

'I'm very sorry to hear that; I hope he didn't suffer too much,' intoned Laxton, a solemn expression on his face.

'He was very brave. He was always telling me that he would get over it and that we would have our Elizabeth back one day,' she told him tearfully as she took out a handkerchief from her apron pocket and dabbed her eyes.

'Is that your husband?' he asked, nodding his head at the photograph on the cabinet.

'It is, bless him,' she confided, her voice full of emotion.

'There is just one thing more Mrs Watling,' the inspector declared as he got to his feet and prepared to leave.

'And what would that be?' she queried, her brow furrowed.

'I would like you to take a blood test and have it sent to forensics at Lincoln police headquarters,' he told her.

'Does this mean that I might see my daughter again?' she asked hopefully as she looked up into the eyes of the tall man in front of her.

'I don't want to get your hopes up too much Mrs Watling. It depends on certain circumstances I'm afraid,' he explained with a slight shake of his head.

With this he made his way out of the conservatory; he paused for a moment as he opened the front door and prepared to leave.

'You will keep in touch with me Inspector?' she said plaintively as he stepped outside the cottage.

Laxton nodded his head and told her that he would indeed keep in touch with her before closing the door behind him; he was deep in thought as he strode up the garden path, climbed into his car and drove off. His brain was working overtime as he went over what had transpired so far. Suddenly he came to decision.

'I think I'll interview the Batleys while I'm in the area,' he told himself, half closing his eyes against the sun as it appeared from behind a heavy cloud.

He checked his watch, it was four fifteen. 'I've just about got time,' he muttered, as he set off for Market Rasen. Putting his foot down on the accelerator he sped up; twenty-five minutes later he entered Market Rasen. After ten minutes of searching for Green Lane, he stopped the car, a look of frustration on his face. An elderly couple walking their dog came by; he wound the window down and called out to them, 'Excuse me.'

The couple came over to him a questioning expression on their faces.

'Can you tell me where Green Lane is please?'

'You are almost on it,' replied the grey-haired man, pointing with his finger. 'Take the next turning on the left then the next turning on the right is Green Lane.'

Laxton thanked the man before following his instructions.

Driving slowly down Green Lane, he eventually came across Oak Cottage. It was an old building that stood well back. Climbing out of the car, he went through a wooden gate and walked down a path through the middle of a well laid out garden; the path led to a wooden weather-beaten door. He reached out and rang the bell. After a couple of minutes the door opened; a small woman who looked to be in her early fifties stood in front of him.

'Mrs Batley?'

'Yes, can I help you?' she said a little sharply.

Laxton introduced himself. She stood back, her attitude visibly softening.

'Please come on in,' she gushed, her stern face changing into a broad smile.

The inspector gave a nod of his head and stepped

through the door. Closing the door, she led him into a large lounge.

'Norman, this is Inspector Laxton,' she told her husband, who had been watching the news on the television. He jumped to his feet and strode across the room his hand held out. Laxton shook it.

'We were told that you would be coming. It's to do with our Jonathan isn't it?'

Laxton nodded his head, telling him, 'Certain facts have come to our notice regarding the abduction of your son in nineteen sixty-eight.'

The tall gaunt man turned to his wife, a look of astonishment on his whiskery face. 'Did you hear that Dorothy? We are going to get our Jonathan back,'

'Whoa, hold on!' exclaimed the inspector, holding his hands up. 'I didn't say that we had located him.'

Dorothy, a look of disappointment on her face, looked up at him. 'So we aren't going to get him back.'

Laxton smiled, telling her with a slight shake of his head, 'It's not as straight forward as that I'm afraid.'

'What have come to see us for then?' queried Norman a little belligerently.

'Well the first thing we've got to have is proof that anyone we have in mind is the right person,' the inspector put to him.

'What do you mean by proof?' asked Dorothy.

'First of all you will have to have a blood test.'

'Where do we have that?'

'You will have to go to the nearest hospital for your blood test then it will have to be sent to Lincoln police headquarters.'

'If we've got the right blood group then we'll get our son back,' said Dorothy.

'Not exactly, there are other factors to be taken into account,' the inspector told her.

'What other factors?' asked Norman.

'Well, has your son got any birth marks that would identify him beyond doubt?'

Norman, his eyes half closed as he cast his mind back, ran his fingers through his thinning hair.

'I don't think he has a birth mark has he Dorothy?' he remarked, turning to his wife.

'If I remember rightly one of his feet was smaller than the other. The doctor told us that he would have the deformity for life,' said Dorothy.

'I reckon that may be enough,' rejoined Laxton as he turned to leave. 'Don't forget to take the blood test,' he told them as he went out of the door.

The inspector pulled the car door shut before settling in his seat; he checked his watch as he fastened his seatbelt – it was five forty-five.

'Looks like I'll be late home again,' he muttered to himself as he started the car and drove off.

The sun was just beginning to dip down over the horizon as he approached Lincoln. Ten minutes later he was pulling into the police station car park.

Bellows glanced up from the paperwork that he was poring over as Laxton walked through the door.

'The chief told me to send you straight in; he's been waiting for you.'

Laxton nodded his head in acknowledgement as he walked across the reception office and opened the chief's door. He was sat behind his desk, his arms folded as the inspector walked in.

'Ah Robert, you are late, I've been waiting for you!' he exclaimed as Laxton pulled up a chair and sat down.

The inspector explained to the chief that as Mrs Watling's home was only a few miles from Market Rasen he had decided to call at the Batleys' home and interview them; he then proceeded to go through the details and results of his investigations during the day.

'Mmm,' muttered Wilberton after he had listened to what Laxton had to say. 'It seems as though we may be finally getting somewhere.'

He went silent for a moment; he was deep in thought as he tapped lightly on the desk top with his fingertips.

'You say that the son that was taken from the Batleys has a slightly deformed foot, that should make the identification much easier.'

Laxton nodded his head in agreement.

Wilberton stroked his chin for a few seconds, deep in thought.

'The blood tests of the three parents should be through some time tomorrow; taking into account what you have told me we should get some results,' he declared, looking across the desk at Laxton as he added, 'I think it would be a good idea if you contacted Rebecca Malling and informed her that you will be visiting her tomorrow morning.'

Laxton reached out for the phone which was on the desk in front of him; he picked it up and dialled a number. A few seconds later he was through.

'Hello is that Rebecca Malling?'

'It is,' replied a young woman's voice on the other end of the phone.

'This is Inspector Laxton. Would it be possible for me to see you tomorrow morning, say about ten o'clock?'

'Yes that will be okay,' the voice replied.

Laxton gave a half smile at the phone as he thanked her.

'I'll make that my first call,' he told the chief as he replaced the phone.

He checked his watch; it was almost six thirty.

'That will about do me for today,' he muttered as he got wearily to his feet.

'See you tomorrow sometime Robert,' declared Wilberton as the inspector went out of the office; he gave a farewell wave to Bellows before pushing open the glass entrance door and leaving.

Black clouds blotted out the setting sun as Laxton made his way to his car and climbed in. He gave a deep sigh before fastening his seatbelt. A few minutes later he set off on the journey back to his cottage in Old Bolingbroke; he tapped his finger on the steering wheel in time with the radio which was belting out a Bill Haley rock and roll tune as he turned off the main road and wended his way through the dark country lanes. He gave a smile as the headlights shone on a rabbit which had just stepped out of the long grass that was growing along the side of the lane and was about make a dash across it, when it suddenly changed its mind and darted back out of sight.

'Sensible rabbit,' he muttered to himself as he took his foot off the brake and accelerated up a slight incline.

It was seven twenty-five when he eventually turned into his driveway. Annie was just closing the door behind her as she prepared to leave.

'I couldn't wait any longer Mr Laxton,' she told him as he switched off the headlights and climbed out of the car.

'That's okay Annie,' he rejoined, a broad smile on his face.

'Your dinner is in the oven,' she called out to him as she mounted her bike and rode off, her broad rump going up and down rhythmically as she pedalled vigorously out of the driveway.

Wearily he went into the cottage. The smell of steak and kidney pie invaded his nostrils as he walked into the kitchen. A few minutes later, after he had opened a can of beer and poured it into a glass, he was tucking in to the inviting meal. After finishing it he patted his stomach.

'That was really something,' he muttered, a satisfied expression on his face as he reached out for his glass of beer and took a long drink.

After finishing his drink off he picked up his plate and glass and placed them in the sink before going upstairs to take a shower. Half an hour later he stretched out on the settee in the lounge, switched on the television and relaxed as he watched the news.

Chapter 6

Laxton stepped out of the door and pulled it shut behind him; he glanced up at the heavy clouds and grimaced as he walked across the drive to his car.

'Looks like another wet day,' he muttered to himself as he settled himself behind the steering wheel. He paused for a moment as he checked his watch. It showed nine o'clock. He reckoned that he would get to Langworth at about nine forty-five. Giving a nod of satisfaction, he reached out and turned on the ignition; a few seconds later he drove out of the gateway. He gave a farewell wave to Annie who was approaching along the lane on his right as he put his foot down and made his way out of Old Bolingbroke; spits of rain were hitting the windscreen as he climbed the hill on the outskirts of the village on his way to his rendezvous with Rebecca Malling. After half an hour of driving through the, by now, heavy rain he arrived at the young woman's residence in Langworth.

Jumping out of the car he made a dash through the

heavy downpour to the front door which opened as he arrived by Rebecca Malling; she had seen him pull into the drive.

'Thank you Miss Malling,' said the inspector as he stepped through the door and into the hallway.

'You are welcome Inspector,' she rejoined with a smile and a nod of her head, as she closed the door behind him.

Leading him into the lounge, she asked him if he would like a coffee as he sat down in one of the easy chairs.

'Yes please,' he told her, with a nod of his head.

Rebecca went into the kitchen and switched the electric kettle on. Laxton made himself comfortable in the chair and clasped his hands in front of him as he cast his eyes appreciatively around the large lounge, taking in the couple of oil paintings hanging on the walls as the rattle of pots could be heard emanating from the kitchen.

After five minutes had gone by Rebecca came through the door carrying a tray with two cups on it.

'Here we are,' she remarked as she entered the lounge, placed the tray on a small table and took a seat opposite the inspector.

'Now then Inspector, what is it you want to see me about?' enquired the young woman as she reached out for her cup of coffee.

Laxton leaned back in his chair, and folded his arms before addressing her. 'First of all Miss Malling, I would like you to take a blood test.'

Rebecca's eyes opened wide, the cup stopping inches from her lips.

'Does this mean that you have come up with something?' she asked, a little hesitantly.

'Well!' exclaimed the inspector, pausing for a few seconds to take a drink of his coffee, before going on to tell her, 'I wouldn't say that we have something concrete to tell you, but we are hoping that the blood test may give us a lead.'

'When and where would you like me to take the test?' enquired Rebecca.

'As soon as possible,' Laxton told her adding, 'I reckon Lincoln County Hospital would be the best place to have it done as we have arranged for the sample to be sent to forensics.'

'I'll get over there straight away,' she declared firmly.

The inspector told her that it would be very helpful if she did this.

'If you are ready now, Miss Malling I can drop you off at the hospital,' he put to her.

'Thank you Inspector, I'll get ready immediately,' she rejoined as she got to her feet, picked up the tray and took it into the kitchen.

Laxton pushed himself up out of the chair and walked to the door, where he waited patiently for her to don her coat. After a quick glance at herself in the hall mirror she was ready to go. Opening the front door she stepped outside followed by the tall detective; a few seconds later they climbed into the car. Laxton glanced out of the corner of his eye to check that she was strapped in before starting the car and driving off. The traffic was pretty heavy as they approached the hospital.

He turned to her as they turned off the main road

and onto the one way system in the hospital grounds.

'I'll drop you off outside the main entrance,' he intoned, before going on to tell her, 'if you explain to the girl at the reception what you are here for she will put you right.'

Rebecca thanked him before disembarking from the car; after giving a farewell wave of her hand she made her way to the entrance which was marked A and E.

The inspector acknowledged the wave of her hand with a nod of his head before driving off. A few minutes later he was pulling into the police station car park. After sitting for a few seconds reflecting on the mornings events he got out of the car and walked across to the entrance. Bellows, who was sat at his desk busy filling in a form, greeted him with a nod and a half smile as he walked through the door.

Laxton gave a nod in return before going to the chief's door, giving a sharp knock on it and walking in.

'Now then Robert,' Wilberton began as the inspector pulled out a chair and sat down. 'Have you anything to add to what we already know?'

Laxton made himself comfortable, before carefully going through the mornings events.

'Mmm,' muttered Wilberton. 'It looks as though things are beginning to move.'

'Well we may have something more definite after we've received the result of the blood samples,' Laxton told him.

'What about the two thousand pound cheques. Have you come up with anything regarding them?' enquired the chief, a questioning frown on his brow.

'I've still got to look into those,' admitted Laxton

with a shake of his head, adding: 'I thought it might be a good idea to wait until after we've received the result of the blood tests.'

Wilberton nodded his head in agreement. 'You are probably right,' he declared.

He ran his fingers slowly up and down the bridge of his nose for a few seconds as he decided on the next move.

'I'll give forensics a ring and check if the parents have been in touch with them,' he muttered as he reached out for the phone and placed it against his ear.

'Hello!' he said loudly. 'Can you put me through to forensics please?'

He drummed on the top of the desk with his forefinger as he waited for a reply; after what seemed an interminable length of time, he was put through.

'Hello is that forensics?' he said into the phone. 'Ahh good. This is Chief Inspector Wilberton here. Have you received the samples of blood from the relatives of the missing children yet?'

'There was another pause before the chief started taking notice.

'Yes I've got that,' he muttered before going on to ask, 'when will you be able to come up with a conclusion?'

After nodding his head at the phone for a few seconds, he muttered his thanks and put the receiver down.

Sitting back in his chair, he took off his glasses, reached out for a piece of tissue paper and polished them; after putting them back on he addressed Laxton, who had been sat with a questioning expression on his face throughout the exchange.

'It seems that forensics have received the blood samples from the two sets of parents that we have contacted so far. I'm afraid there wasn't a match. They are waiting for the blood samples from Rebecca Malling so that they can check if her sample matches,' he told him.

'I've just dropped Miss Malling off at the hospital about half an hour ago,' remarked Laxton before going on to tell the chief, 'it shouldn't be too long before her blood sample reaches forensics. If it proves to be a match it could give us a lead as to the whereabouts of the other children that also went missing.'

'Hold your horses Robert!' exclaimed Wilberton, holding up his hands. 'Don't jump the gun!'

Laxton leaned forward in his seat, his chin jutting out aggressively. 'Well it is possible,' he countered.

'Yes I agree, but we are a long way from any firm conclusions yet,' replied the chief, shaking his head.

At that moment Bellows came through the door carrying a tray and the obligatory mugs of coffee. They both nodded their thanks as he placed the mugs on the desk in front of them before retreating. Laxton reached out and picked up one of the hot drinks, blew on it and took a tentative sip before putting a pertinent point to the chief:

'If we discover that Rebecca Malling's blood matches a sample from one of the couples who have lost their child then it follows that the other parents could possibly also have lost their children the same way, don't you think?'

Wilberton, who had been taking a drink of his

coffee, placed his mug back on the desk top, before stroking his chin reflectively as he thought over what the inspector had said.

'You may have something there Robert,' he replied. His voice lowering in volume, he added, 'If this is the case, we'll set about tracing the people who cashed the cheques. We should be able to do that through the bank that issued them.'

Suddenly the phone on Wilberton's desk rang out sharply. He reached out, picked it up and held it to his ear.

'Hello, Chief Inspector Wilberton here,' he said somewhat solemnly.

His face took on a serious expression as he nodded his head at the phone.

'Yes I've got that,' he muttered into the mouthpiece.

After a few seconds of further listening, he said, 'Thank you.'

He had a thoughtful look on his face as he placed the phone back on its cradle.

Laxton, who was in the process of taking another drink of his coffee, looked at him questioningly over the rim of his mug.

'What was that all about?' he asked as he placed what was left of his drink back on the desk top.

The chief chewed on his bottom lip for a few seconds before telling him, 'That was forensics. It seems that they have a match regarding Rebecca Malling.'

'Did they give any indication as to who the natural parents may be?' enquired Laxton as he finished off his drink, leaned over and placed the empty mug on the desk.

Wilberton shook his head negatively, before going on to explain, 'It seems that Miss Malling has a rare blood group. Until they have a little more proof they won't be able to say for certain who the natural parents may be.' He paused for a few seconds before going on to explain to him, 'It seems that although having such a rare blood group cuts down the odds somewhat, it isn't a one hundred per cent certainty that one of them is the parent.'

The inspector, deep in thought, mulled over what the chief had said for a couple of seconds before telling him, 'One of the parents that I interviewed, who had lost a child around the same time that Miss Malling was abducted told me that she had been involved in an accident which had injured the daughter that she had lost.'

Wilberton leaned forward, his elbows on the desk in front of him as he absorbed the information that Laxton had given him, then he instructed him to get in touch with the people involved and arrange a meeting at the Lincoln police station headquarters where they could sort out 'who belonged to who'.

The middle aged nurse at the hospital withdrew the needle from an apprehensive Rebecca Malling's arm.

'There my dear that wasn't so bad was it?' she said a broad smile on her face as she placed a small wad of cotton wool over the puncture in her arm and stuck it down with a strip of sticking plaster.

Rebecca, a look of relief on her face, got to her

feet and thanked the nurse before asking her what would happen now.

'Well we've had instructions to send this sample to forensics straight away, as the police say they need it as soon as possible,' she explained to her, a serious expression on her round face.

Rebecca again thanked her before putting on her coat and opening the door; making her way along the corridor, she exited the hospital via the double glass entrance doors. A bus with Langworth displayed on the front of it was just entering the hospital grounds as she walked to the bus stop. A few minutes later she was on her way home. The journey was quite a pleasant one as the bus wended its way through the open countryside in the warm sunshine on its way to the attractive village of Langworth. There was a sense of excitement in her breast at the possibility of seeing her real mother. What was she like? Did she resemble her? Did she have any brothers and sisters? She shook her head in bewilderment as the thoughts ran through her head.

After twenty minutes had gone by the bus duly arrived at Langworth. Jumping off, she quickly covered the hundred yards or so to her home. Entering the bungalow, she closed the door behind her and gingerly took off her coat; being careful not to knock the protective patch that covered the tender spot where the needle had entered her arm.

Hanging her coat in the closet that was situated in the hallway, she went into the kitchen and put the kettle on. There was an eerie feeling about the place that she just couldn't quite place. It was as if her mum was in the kitchen with her as she placed a teabag in the cup and poured the hot water into it. She cast her eyes around the front room, half expecting to see the back of her dad's bald head sticking up over the back of the settee as she entered. She gave an involuntary shudder as she sat in one of the easy chairs and took a sip of her tea. She felt very lonely. Suddenly the phone rang, almost making her spill her tea. She put the cup down and reached out for the phone.

'Hello?' she breathed into the mouthpiece.

'Is that you Becky?' a familiar voice enquired.

She gave a sigh of relief, it was her boyfriend Joseph.

'Hi Joe,' she greeted him, her face breaking into a broad smile as she added, 'am I glad to hear from you?'

'You are all right aren't you darling?' he put to her concernedly.

'W-ell,' she said a little hesitantly. 'It is beginning to get a little too much for me.'

'Do you reckon I should come down there and keep you company?' he muttered into the phone.

'That would be really nice Joe,' she told him huskily.

'Right that's settled then,' he replied firmly, telling her, 'I'll jump in the car and be with you in a few hours Becky.'

A thrill went through her at the thought of her boyfriend joining her, as she put the phone down and finished drinking her cup of tea.

She checked the time by the old grandfather clock that stood the corner of the room. It was two o'clock. She was beginning to feel hungry. Going back into the kitchen, she ran her eyes over the offerings in the fridge. Taking out a half pound pack of butter, a loaf and a few slices of cheese that were on a plate, she proceeded to make herself a few sandwiches. She was almost through the last of the sandwiches when the phone rang again; picking up the receiver she put it to her ear and spoke into it.

'Hello,' she said.

'Is that Rebecca Malling?' a man's voice enquired.

The young woman swallowed a couple of times to clear her throat before replying in the affirmative.

'This is Inspector Laxton speaking. When would it be convenient for you to come to the Lincoln Headquarters to be interviewed?' the voice enquired.

She paused for a moment as she thought over the inspector's request.

'Would tomorrow morning, say at around eleven o'clock be okay?' she put to him.

'Yes, I reckon that would do nicely,' he replied.

'Oh by the way Inspector Laxton,' she butted in before he could put the phone down, 'have you come up with any clues as to who my true parents may be?'

There was silence on the other end of the phone for a few seconds before the inspector spoke again in a somewhat measured tone of voice, 'Young lady tomorrow may be an eventful day for you.'

Rebecca's hand went to her mouth. 'Are – are you telling me that you have found my parents?' she gasped.

'That is something we are hoping to find out tomorrow morning,' he told her before putting the phone down.

She stood for a moment, transfixed, as she gazed at the mouthpiece in her hand. Putting it back on its cradle she turned and walked slowly into the lounge, what remained of her sandwich was forgotten as she flopped down on the settee. Her eyes were unseeing as she reached out for her cup of tea, put it to her lips and finished it off; her mind was in a whirl as she tried to envisage what her parents might look like. Rebecca was brought abruptly out of her trance by the shrill ringing of the phone again, getting to her feet she went into the hallway and picked it up. It was her uncle Brian.

'I'm just ringing to let you know that I have been in touch with the mortuary and made arrangements for the burial of your mum and dad. That is of course if it suits you,' he told her in a low voice full of feeling.

'That's very good of you, Uncle,' she told him, adding that she wouldn't have known how to go about it anyway.

'That's what I figured,' he replied, before going on to tell her that he would get in touch with her at a later date after he had everything organised.

After thanking him for his help she placed the phone down and walked slowly into the lounge. Her mind was in turmoil as the events of the past week or so filled her thoughts.

Flopping down on the comfortable settee she laid her head back on the arm and closed her eyes; pictures of her mum and dad appeared out of the blackness as the welcome relief of sleep overcame her. She was suddenly awakened to the sound of the front door bursting open and a man's voice calling out, 'Becky, I'm here.'

Footsteps could be heard making their way along the hallway into the kitchen as she shook the cobwebs out of her head.

'Where are you darling?' the voice called out.

'I'm in the lounge Joseph,' she called out excitedly, as she jumped to her feet and made a beeline for the door.

At that moment it swung open, Joseph was standing in the doorway in front of her, a broad smile on his face as he held out his arms.

'It's really good to see you Joseph,' she sighed, tears rolling down her cheeks as she flung herself into his strong embrace.

'Don't cry Becky,' he mumbled, burying his face in her long dark hair and almost crushing her with his arms.

'It was such a shock when I got home,' she sobbed, shaking her head. 'Without my mum and dad the place seemed so empty.'

Joseph reached into his pocket and pulled out a large handkerchief and held it out, telling her, 'Wipe your eyes darling.'

'Thank you,' she mumbled as she took it from him and dabbed her eyes and nose.

He reached out with his thumb and forefinger, tilted her chin and looked down into her large watery blue eyes. 'Be brave Becky, I'll be here to help you all I can.'

She took a deep breath and compressed her lips. 'I know that I've got to get over it Joseph,' she told him determinedly.

'That's the spirit,' he whispered encouragingly as

she stuck her chin out firmly.

'Uncle Brian has just been in touch with me. He has assured me that he will sort out the arrangements for the funeral,' she told him.

'That's good of him,' said Joseph, putting his arm around her shoulders and giving her an encouraging squeeze. 'That should take care of a lot of the hassle for you.'

She nodded her head in agreement, but her eyes were still clouded over.

'There is something else worrying you isn't there?' Joseph put to her.

Rebecca nodded her head before going on to tell him about the tabs from the cheques for two thousand pounds each, that she had found among her parents belongings in the box and the implication that they were payment for her adoption.

'Adoption?' intoned Joseph, a questioning expression on his face as he sat up straight on his chair with the shock of what she had told him.

'Yes,' she whispered almost inaudibly, before going on to explain to him that she had handed them over to inspector Laxton and that he was going to look into them.

'When will you find out the truth about your parents?'

She gave a shrug of her shoulders before telling him, 'I have an appointment at the police headquarters tomorrow morning at eleven o'clock. They might have come up with something helpful,' she explained.

Joseph checked his watch, it was five p.m.

'I'll take my things into the bedroom,' he told her as he picked up his case, gave her a peck on the cheek and walked out of the lounge.

'I'll fix you something to eat,' she called after him.

'Don't bother Becky, I'm going to take you out for a meal,' he rejoined as he disappeared into the bedroom and closed the door behind him.

An hour later Joseph, with Becky suitably attired by his side, was steering the car out of the driveway and onto the road. They had gone a couple of miles when they came across the 'olde worlde' Cock and Hen public house. The good looking young couple took a seat at one of the tables in the dining area. They were running their eyes over the menu when a waitress came to them pad in hand and asked them what they would be having.

'I'll have scampi and chips,' said Becky.

'I'll have the same,' declared Joseph adding, 'and two glasses of wine.'

The meals turned out to be really enjoyable and the two returned back at the bungalow in a much happier frame of mind. After talking over in detail, the happenings of the last few days they decided to have an early night in readiness for their appointment at police headquarters the following day.

Chapter 7

Laxton was deep in thought as he carefully ran the razor over his jawline. After drying himself he walked out of the bathroom, made his way downstairs and into the kitchen, where he put the kettle on.

Reaching out he placed a couple of slices of bread in the toaster as the kettle boiled. A few minutes later he was tucking in to his somewhat meagre breakfast. Quickly drinking his coffee, he got to his feet and donned his coat before going outside and climbing into his car in readiness for his journey to Lincoln Police Headquarters. He lowered the nearside window as Annie his cleaner entered the driveway on her bike, a beaming smile on her round face.

'Feed Horatio Annie,' he called out to her as she clumsily dismounted.

'Leave it to me Mister Laxton,' she assured him over her shoulder as she leaned her old bike against the side of the cottage wall.

Raising his hand in a farewell gesture, he exited the property. The sun was rising in a clear blue sky as he accelerated along the lane and out of the village. He gave a deep sigh of contentment as he put his foot down and climbed the hill out of Old Bolingbroke; fields on either side of him as far as the eye could see were a carpet of bright yellow.

'It seems as though the local farmers have really took to the growing of rapeseed,' he muttered to himself as he approached the junction of the main road to Lincoln; after another five minutes of driving, he joined the traffic on the busy highway.

Half an hour later the Three Sisters of Lincoln Cathedral came into view as they jutted into the sky; the inspector took little notice, his mind was on the forthcoming meeting with the parents of the missing children. Another ten minutes went by as he navigated his way through the heavy traffic, eventually arriving at police headquarters car park. He gave a loud groan as he unfastened his seatbelt and stretched his arms out wide; giving a deep sigh, he climbed out of the car and went into the outer office. Sergeant Bellows was busy checking through some documents; he looked up as the inspector walked through the door.

'Is the chief in yet?' Laxton enquired, leaning his elbow on the counter.

Bellows, a broad smile in his round face, nodded his head. 'He's been in a good half an hour,' he chuckled, before going on to inform him: 'He's waiting for you.'

The inspector thanked him before striding across the outer office and opening the chief's door.

Wilberton, who had been poring over a document, straightened up in his chair as Laxton entered the room. Closing the door behind him, he pulled out a chair from under the table in front of the chief and sat down.

'Now then,' exclaimed the chief as he leaned forward in his chair and placed his elbows on the desk. 'Let's go over today's agenda.'

The inspector gave a nod of his head as Wilberton opened a drawer in front of him and took out a sheet of paper; after studying it for a few seconds he turned to Laxton, telling him, 'At the present time, according to forensics, the nearest we've got to a match in the blood groups put forward by the parents who have lost their children is by one Mary Watling.'

Laxton sat up in his seat as he was about to comment.

The chief held up his hand before he could say anything.

'Taking into account the facts that we have received, the results, although promising are still not conclusive,' he explained.

'Surely if they have the same rare blood group that should be enough,' Laxton put to him.

Wilberton smiled before shaking his head negatively.

'It may look that way Robert, but even though the group is a rare one, there are still many thousands with that same blood group,' he told him.

'That may be so Chief but it does cut out the ones that aren't in that group,' explained Laxton.

Wilberton, deep in thought, went over the facts in his mind before turning to Laxton.

'I agree,' he replied with a nod of his head. 'But we are going to need more than that before we can say for certain which child belongs to whom.'

He raised his arm and looked at his wrist watch; it was nine thirty.

'Sergeant Bellows,' he called out loudly.

The office door opened and the sergeant stepped in. 'Yes Chief?'

'What time have you arranged for Mrs Watling to be here?' he enquired.

'Eleven o'clock,' replied the sergeant, adding, 'the same time as Miss Rebecca Malling.'

The chief thanked him then called out as he was going out of the door, 'Send two coffees in please.'

Laxton, who had been listening intently to what the chief had been saying, leaned forward, his elbows on his knees. 'What about the other parents, aren't we going to interview them?' he enquired, his brow furrowed questioningly.

'We can leave them until a later date,' Wilberton told him.

A couple of minutes later Constable Billings came through the door carrying a tray with two mugs of coffee on it. The lanky nineteen-year-old placed the tray on the desk.

'Thank you Constable,' said Wilberton crisply as the young man turned to go out of the room.

Laxton smiled his thanks before reaching out, picking up one of the mugs and taking a tentative sip at the hot liquid.

'Now then Robert,' declared the chief, clasping his hands in front of him. 'What do you think would be our best approach regarding Mrs Watling?'

Laxton chewed on his bottom lip for a few

seconds as he thought over what the chief had said.

'First of all I think it would be a good idea to ascertain that she is the mother of Rebecca Malling before proceeding any further,' he put to him.

'Hmm, that's going to be easier said than done,' replied Wilberton.

At that moment a female voice could be heard coming from the outer office; seconds later the door opened and Bellows head showed round it.

'A Mrs Watling here to see you sir,' he announced.

'Send her in Sergeant,' Wilberton told him.

A moment later the smartly dressed woman stepped into the office, a nervous smile playing on her face as she reached out and shook hands with the two policemen.

'Good morning Mrs Watling,' the chief greeted her, a broad smile on his face as he got to his feet and shook her small hand before telling her, 'I'm Chief Inspector Wilberton.' He added with a nod of his head towards the inspector, 'You and Inspector Laxton have already met.'

She gave a nod of recognition as she acknowledged her earlier meeting with the inspector, who had jumped out of his chair and offered it to her.

'Thank you,' she said graciously. She sat down and adjusted her rather short skirt before turning to Wilberton and asking him somewhat straightforwardly, 'Now then Chief Inspector, What have you got to tell me?'

Wilberton sat back in his chair, folded his arms and plucked at the lobe of his left ear, his eyes half closed as he thought over his approach. After a few seconds he directed his gaze at the woman in front of him.

'First of all Mrs Watling, we have to ascertain beyond doubt that you are the true parent of the young woman who has been in touch with us,' he explained to her in a serious tone of voice before going on to tell her that the results of the blood test had come through.

Marjory Watling suddenly straightened up in her chair, her hands clasped tightly; she had a questioning expression on her face as she leaned towards Wilberton.

'And what do they say?' she asked, almost in a whisper.

The chief leaned forward, his elbows on his knees and looked the woman straight in the eyes.

'We have been informed that the blood group of the young woman matches your blood group Mrs Watling,' he told her.

There was a deep intake of breath as the implication of what she had just heard sunk in.

'Does this mean that she is my daughter?' she stammered, her face going white at the shock of what she had heard.

'Not exactly!' exclaimed Wilberton, before going on to explain to her. 'Lots of people will have that same blood group Mrs Watling, even though it may be rare.'

Laxton, who had been listening to the altercation, butted in. 'You will need to come up with more proof I'm afraid,' he informed her.

She turned to him, a questioning expression on her face. 'What do you mean by proof?' she put to him, a little abruptly.

At that moment the door opened and Bellows

bobbed his head round it.

'Rebecca Malling is in the outer office Chief. She's got her boyfriend with her,' he announced.

'Send them in Sergeant,' he called out, adding, 'oh and bring a couple of chairs in will you?'

The young couple stepped into the chief's office followed by the sergeant and constable Billings carrying a chair each. After they had taken a seat they were introduced to the officers and Marjory Watling. The two women's eyes were locked for a few seconds; they both felt a strange bondage as they clasped hands.

'Would you like a coffee?' Wilberton put to them.

The young couple nodded their heads.

'Er, tea for me please,' said Marjory Watling, a little apologetically.

Laxton a serious expression on his face, addressed her. 'When I last interviewed you there was a mention of an accident which occurred when the daughter that you lost, was about two years old.'

Marjory Watling compressed her lips together for a moment before going on to repeat her story of the accident.

'I stepped down from a stool in the kitchen, my daughter Elizabeth, was playing on the mat; she screamed out in pain as I trod on her right hand.'

She was silent for a few seconds as she glanced down guiltily at her clasped hands before telling them in a voice full of feeling, 'I was wearing high-heeled shoes. My husband George picked her up and carried her to the car; we took her to Accident and Emergency at the local hospital. The on-duty doctor examined Elizabeth's damaged hand and told us that he was going to send her to the x-ray department.'

At that moment Billings came in carrying a tray with drinks. They thanked him as he placed it on the chief's desk and withdrew.

'You were saying Mrs Watling?' remarked the chief.

'Well after she returned from x-ray we were informed that she had broken the knuckle in her middle finger,' she declared with a shrug of her shoulders.

She reached out and picked up her cup of tea and took a drink before adding, 'I asked the doctor if it would be okay when it healed up.'

'What did he say?' enquired the chief.

'He told me that she would always have a deformity in her hand,' she declared, her voice breaking with emotion.

There was a deep intake of breath from Rebecca as she heard the facts.

'Can you hold out your right hand Rebecca?' requested Laxton.

The young woman was in a trance as she pulled back her coat sleeve and held out her right hand. Laxton took hold of the hand and studied it for a couple of seconds. The middle finger was shorter than the finger on either side of it.

'Can I see your left hand?' he asked her.

She nodded her head as she complied with his request and held it out beside the other one.

Laxton matched them up. There was no deformity. It was obvious that Rebecca's right hand had suffered an injury. He sat back and looked deeply at the two women before turning to Marjory Watling a smile playing on his lips as he told her, 'Mrs Watling, your daughter.'

The two women, shaking their heads in disbelief, looked deep into the eyes of the other; tears rolled down their cheeks as they embraced. Rebecca's boyfriend Joseph put his arm around them both and hugged them affectionately.

'Well, that's one pair we've managed to match up, now we'll see what we can do about the others,' announced Wilberton, as he got to his feet and escorted the trio out of the office.

He was stroking his chin thoughtfully as he walked slowly back into his office. Laxton, his arms folded, sat waiting patiently for him to return.

'Robert!' he exclaimed as he closed the door behind him and made his way to his seat behind the desk. 'What do you suggest we should do now to discover the identity of the abductors of these children?'

Laxton leaned forward, resting his elbows on his knees.

'Chief it seems to me that the only lead we've got up to now, is through the tabs from the cheques,' he suggested.

Wilberton sucked on his top lip for a few seconds as he thought over the suggestion that the inspector had put to him. After a slight pause he reached out for the phone and dialled the number of the bank in question, which was situated in the centre of Lincoln.

'Hello, this is Chief Inspector Wilberton of the Lincoln Police Force,' he began, then paused for a moment before going on. 'Can you tell me if one of my officers could have a word with you regarding a rather private matter?'

A couple of minutes went by as he nodded his head at the mouthpiece.

'Yes I've got that,' he said, giving a half smile at the phone before placing it back on its rest and turning to Laxton who had a questioning expression on his face.

'Robert, the bank manager says he will see you this afternoon.'

'Did he say what time he would see me?' enquired Laxton.

'Yes, he said he would be available at around two o'clock,' replied the chief, giving a slight nod of his head, before calling out at the top of his voice, 'Bellows!'

A couple of seconds later the door opened and the sergeant's head popped round it.

'Yes sir!' he said crisply.

Wilberton looked at him over the rim of his glasses.

'Get me the cheque tabs that Miss Malling left with us, will you?' he instructed him.

Bellows returned with the aforesaid tabs, which were in an envelope, he put them on the desk in front of Wilberton, with a, 'There you are Chief,' before leaving.

Wilberton picked up the envelope and handed it to Laxton.

The inspector took the envelope from him and put it in his pocket, before placing his hands on his knees and pushing himself upright. He gave a quick glance at his watch; it showed twelve forty-five. He had just placed his hand on the doorknob when Wilberton called after him: 'Oh I almost forgot to tell you. I want you to take PC Billings with you.'

Laxton stopped in his tracks as he gave the chief a disbelieving look.

'I know – I know!' exclaimed Wilberton, raising his right hand, before going on to explain. 'It seems he has taken the appropriate intelligence tests before applying for plain clothes duty and the powers that be, have instructed me to give him a chance.'

Laxton shook his head; for the last two years Billings had been chief tea masher.

'Oh he is a good lad,' he told himself, 'but…' He left his thoughts unfinished.

'Ok Chief I'll give the young man go,' he said a little reluctantly before he stepped out of the office and closed the door behind him.

He called Bellows over and told him of Billings' ambitions.

'Yes, he's told me, he says being a plain-clothed detective is something he's always wanted,' replied the big sergeant.

Where is young Billings?' enquired Laxton.

'In the back office,' Bellows told him, indicating with his thumb.

Laxton gave nod of his head and made his way to the office that the sergeant had indicated.

The young man was sat at a desk filling a form in; he looked up as the inspector came through the door.

'Come along Constable, you'll be working with me from now on.'

Twenty-four year old Billings' blue eyes lit up as he sprang to his feet.

'That's great news Inspector,' he enthused. 'I've

always dreamed of joining the plain clothes division.'

Laxton smiled as he cast his mind back to when he was introduced to the job; as he remembered he was just as keen as this young man.

'Come on let's have you then,' he put to him a little sharply.

'Shall I need to change out of my uniform and into plain clothes?' he enquired as he followed the inspector through the outer office.

'You'll be okay for today,' he told him.

Bellows pulled Laxton to one side as Billings carried on to the door.

'Robert,' he whispered in his ear. 'You'll be okay with Alan, he will be an asset to you. He's a lot sharper than you think.'

Laxton gave a nod of his head as he followed the younger man out of the door.

Billings ranged himself alongside the inspector as they walked across the station car park. At six foot two he was only an inch shorter than Laxton, but there the similarity ended, his lean, almost gawky figure giving the impression of a bean pole.

The inspector glanced at Billings out of the corner of his eye before tossing him the car keys and instructing him, 'You drive Alan.'

The young constable, visibly pleased at the first name term, deftly caught the bunch of keys, before climbing behind the steering wheel, starting the car and carefully driving off.

'Where to Inspector?' he enquired as he joined the heavy traffic.

Laxton checked his watch; it was almost one

o'clock.

'I reckon a bite to eat would be just about right,' he suggested.

'I know just the place,' rejoined Billings. A few minutes later he turned off the main road and into the countryside; two hundred yards along a country lane he pulled on to the car park of an old white washed pub. A sign hanging outside the pub depicted a red cockerel stretching its neck; underneath it in capitals were the words – The Crowing Cock.

'This is it!' exclaimed the constable as he opened the car door and stuck out a long leg as he prepared to climb out.

Laxton slammed the car door shut and stood on the gravelled surface for a few seconds as he cast his eyes over the ivy covered building.

'I agree Alan, it really does look attractive,' he commented, a look of approval on his face as he followed Billings to the pub entrance.

A blackboard at the back of the bar advertised the day's menu. The star attraction being: Lamb chops, roast and boiled potatoes, peas and cabbage.

Underneath it was the price… Three pounds fifty.

The barman who could have stood in as Oliver Hardy, thought Laxton, waddled towards them.

'What can I do for you gents?' he wheezed, as he wiped the bar top with a cloth.

Laxton nodded his head at the board behind the barman. 'We'll have the lamb chops with all the trimmings,' he told him.

The barman went over to an aperture in the wall at the back of the bar and called out, 'Two lamb chops

Doris!'

Billings leaned over and whispered in Laxton's ear. 'I haven't got enough money,' he said, a note of desperation in his voice.

The inspector lifted his left hand, silencing him.

'It's on me,' he told his younger partner, a half smile on his face.

'I can't let you pay out like that,' rejoined Billings, vigorously shaking his head, his thick mop of black hair flopping over his forehead.

Laxton turned and looked the young man in the eyes; he nodded appreciatively as he saw the honesty shining out of them.

'How much have you got?' he asked.

Billings shrugged his shoulders before telling him a little apologetically that he only had three pounds on him.

'You get the drinks,' Laxton instructed him in a low voice.

The constable edged up to the bar and lifted his hand to attract the barman who had gone to serve a customer.

'Two beers?' he called out as he caught the barman's attention.

'Er, make that two pints of shandy,' said Laxton, correcting him, before explaining that they didn't partake in alcoholic drinks on duty.

A somewhat chastened Billings paid for the drinks before carrying them to a vacant table. Laxton paid for the meals and joined him.

'Where are we headed for after we leave here?' enquired Billings over the sound of an elderly couple operating a fruit machine as they waited for the meal to be served up.

'Our first stop will be the National Bank in Lincoln,' he told him.

At that moment a young, attractive waitress approached them carrying a tray.

'Here you are gentlemen,' she trilled as she placed the tray on the table before picking up the two heaped plate and placing them in front of the two officers.

'Thank you,' they both said in unison as they picked up their knives and forks and tucked in to the tasty looking meal with gusto.

Fifteen minutes later they leaned back, their plates empty. Laxton patted his stomach.

'I really enjoyed that,' he declared as the waitress approached them again.

'Do you require anything else?' she enquired.

'No!' exclaimed the two men with a shake of their heads, then, thanking her for a most satisfactory meal they got to their feet and left.

A few minutes later, with Billings again at the wheel, they made their way back to Lincoln. Laxton checked his watch again; it was half past one.

'That gives us thirty minutes,' he muttered almost to himself, as his young partner concentrated on his driving.

Twenty minutes later they were turning into the somewhat small car park which was situated at the rear of the bank. After parking up they strolled around to the front and entered through the glass doors; they stood in the centre of the reception area for a few seconds to get their bearings. Laxton turned his attention to the small queue of four customers who were waiting to be served. He was just about to join it when a pretty young female bank clerk, seeing their uncertainty, approached the two officers.

'Can I help you gentlemen?' she enquired sweetly.

Laxton explained to her that they had an appointment with the manager.

'Just give me a couple of seconds, sir,' she told him as she turned away and went to an office that was situated at the rear of the bank, after a knock on the door she walked into the office.

Laxton leaned his elbow on the long counter, his fingers intertwined as he waited patiently for her to return.

Eventually she came out of the office; there was a smile on her face as she told them that Mr Mulbeck, the manager, would see them now.

Walking round the end of the counter the two tall officers followed her to the manager's office.

Opening the frosted glass door, she invited them in.

Laxton and Billings both acknowledged the young woman with a smile and a nod of their heads before entering the office.

'Come in gentlemen,' said the manager exuberantly as he indicated with his hand, 'take a seat.'

After giving them time to settle down in the two chairs opposite him and introduce themselves, he leaned forward exposing his bald patch and enquired, 'Now what can I do for you Inspector?'

Laxton paused for a moment before reaching into his pocket and taking out the envelope.

'Can you tell me if it is possible to trace these?' he

put to the red-haired manager as he took out the tabs and placed them on the desk in front of him.

John Mulbeck reached out for his glasses which were on his desk, putting them on he picked up the tabs and studied them. He stroked his gingery, somewhat straggly moustache for a few seconds before expressing his opinion. 'I'm sure it's possible,' he declared, adding with a slight shake of his head, 'but it's going to be bloody difficult Mr Laxton. The problem is that they were issued so long ago.'

'Do you think that you will be able to trace them?' repeated the inspector, a note of urgency in his voice.

Mulbeck shrugged his shoulders.

'It's hard to say offhand,' he muttered before adding, 'I'll see what we can do.'

The inspector got to his feet and thanked him before he and his young partner prepared to exit the office. Mulbeck walked round the desk and shook hands with the two officers.

'Leave it with me Inspector. I'll do my best,' he declared solemnly.

'When do you estimate that you may have some results?' enquired Laxton.

Mulbeck, a studious expression on his face, plucked on his rather chubby bottom lip as he thought over the inspector's query.

'All being well, I will probably have heard something by tomorrow morning,' was the reply.

Laxton nodded his head in acquiescence before walking out of the manager's office followed by Billings.

'Alan,' he said as he and his young partner exited

the bank and made their way to where the car was parked. 'I feel we are finally getting somewhere.'

Ten minutes later they arrived back at head office; Billings confidently parked the big car before handing the keys over to Laxton.

Bellows, who was sat at a table at the rear of the office, was in the process of filling in some paperwork, he looked up at the two men as they came through the door.

'Is the chief alone?' queried the inspector as he leaned his elbows on the long counter.

Bellows nodded his balding head.

The two officers turned to go to the chief's office door.

'Any chance of a coffee Sarge?' asked Billings somewhat cockily, as Laxton reached out for the door handle.

Bellows, stern-faced, compressed his lips before addressing the young man. 'I'll send them in,' was his sharp reply. He hadn't yet accepted his ex-office boy as an equal.

Wilberton was pacing back and forth as the two men entered his office.

'Robert, I've been thinking that it may be a good idea to have another talk to the other parents who have lost their children,' he declared, stopping in his tracks.

Laxton gave a shrug of his shoulders.

'I can't see that doing any good Chief,' he rejoined, adding: 'They didn't seem to have a clue as to who took their children the last time we interviewed them.'

'Maybe there is something that they may have noticed that they have overlooked,' piped up Billings confidently.

'That's just what I was thinking Constable,' intoned Wilberton with an almost imperceptible nod of his slightly greying head as he took his seat behind his desk.

Laxton cast an irritating glance at his young partner. The last thing he needed at the moment was to be asking futile questions. At that moment Bellows came in with three coffees on a tray.

'Here you are gents,' he announced as he placed the tray on the desk and gave the young constable a mean look before retracing his steps and leaving.

The chief, a determined expression on his face, took a sip at his coffee before turning to Laxton.

'Robert I want you to interview again, all the parents that are involved,' he reiterated.

'What about the parents of the boy that was abducted... Mr and Mrs Batley?' rejoined the inspector as he reached out and placed his empty mug on the tray, adding, as he dabbed his mouth with his handkerchief: 'It was only a couple of days ago that I last interviewed them and I did come up with quite a lot of information regarding the proof that is needed to provide a match.'

Wilberton twiddled with his fingers for moment or two before telling him, 'Yes you've got something there but I still think it would be a good idea to have another talk to the three couples who are involved.'

'Can I check their addresses?' enquired Billings.

Wilberton nodded his head before sitting back in his chair and pulling out a drawer in his desk.

After a few seconds shuffling around the drawer he muttered, 'Here we are!' as he produced a sheet of

A4. On it were written all the addresses of the families that were involved in the kidnapping.

Billings jotted them down in his notebook.

Laxton checked his watch, it was three forty-five.

'It's too late to do anything today Chief; we'll look into it first thing tomorrow morning,' he declared as he got to his feet.

'Hmm, you are right Robert; it is a bit late,' he put to the inspector as he and Billings were about to leave. 'Before you go I'll give them a ring to arrange for them to meet up with the other couples involved.'

Picking up the phone he dialled the number. After a few seconds it was answered.

'Hello is that Mr Batley?' he said rather loudly. There was pause before he spoke again. 'This is Chief Inspector Wilberton of the Lincoln Police Department, I'm ringing to inform you that two of my officers will be coming to interview you again tomorrow morning in connection with the child that was abducted from you.'

There was another pause; the chief glanced up at the ceiling, his lips compressed as he listened to Mr Batley's reply.

'I would say about ten o'clock, if that's all right with you,' he informed him.

He nodded his head at the phone before putting it back on its rest.

'He says he will watch out for you,' he informed them.

The inspector and his young partner walked out of the door with a, 'See you some time tomorrow Chief.'

'Now then Alan we'd better drop you off,' said

Laxton as they fastened their seatbelts.

'By the way, where do you live?'

'Blenheim Place,' the young man replied, adding: 'Number twenty-six.'

Laxton looked across at him a questioning frown on his forehead.

'And where would that be situated?'

'Oh, sorry, er, Wragby,' rejoined Billings hesitantly.

'That's handy!' exclaimed the inspector as he accelerated out of the station car park. 'It's on my way home.'

The journey continued in silence as they wended their way through the busy traffic in the centre of Lincoln. After negotiating the roundabout on the outskirts of the city, Laxton turned to his young partner. 'Do you live with your parents?'

Billings shrugged his shoulders, before telling Laxton that he lived with his mother and sister.

'Has your dad passed away?' enquired the inspector, a solemn tone to his voice.

The young man laughed and shook his head. 'No nothing like that.'

He paused for a few seconds before going on reluctantly to explain that his father had left his mother, sister Belinda, and him ten years ago.

'So you are the head of the household,' Laxton put to him, a half smile on his face.

'No!' he exclaimed, returning the smile. 'In the family pecking order I come just in front of our Lady.'

'Your Lady?' rejoined the inspector, a questioning expression on his face.

The young man threw his head back and laughed before telling Laxton that Lady was a Jack Russell terrier.

Laxton took his eyes off the road for a second and checked his watch; it was four thirty. They were just approaching the outskirts of Wragby.

'Take the second turning on the left,' instructed Billings, pointing with his finger.

Laxton nodded his head. A few seconds later they were travelling along a tree-lined road. *Quite pleasant*, he thought to himself as he dropped down into third.

'Now the next one on your right,' piped up the young man.

The inspector slowed down as he turned the car into Blenheim Place, a few seconds later he stopped outside number sixteen. Climbing out of the car, Alan led him through the gate and along a path that cut through the centre of the lawn to the front door.

'Hi Mum,' he called out as they stepped into the hallway.

'Alan,' his mum called out from the rear of the smart, semi-detached house. 'What have I told you about using the front door? My carpet won't be worth…'

She stopped, her mouth open in surprise as she walked into the lounge to be confronted by the tall inspector.

'This is Inspector Laxton, Mum I'm going to be working with him from now on,' Alan told her.

'I, I'm sorry I spoke like that Inspector. I don't know what you must think of me,' she said, flushing a little with embarrassment.

Laxton, a broad smile on his face, raised his hand.

'No Mrs Billings you were right to sound off,' he chuckled as he reached out and took hold of her small hard-worked hand.

'Pleased to meet you,' he declared.

The slim, good looking, dark-haired woman nodded her head slightly before reaching up and pushing a wayward lock of hair back over her shoulder.

'Are you going to stop for a cup of tea Inspector?'

'Er Robert,' he corrected her, adding, 'Yes that would be nice.'

'Call me Marie,' she instructed him, a little huskily as she turned to go into the kitchen.

Laxton sat down and relaxed on the settee, Alan sat in one of the easy chairs opposite him. A low growl emanating from a box in the corner of the room, greeted the inspector as he shuffled his backside to make himself more comfortable. The small bundle of brown and white jumped out of the box and walked menacingly towards him, her hackles raised. Alan reached out and picked up a magazine from a stack that were on a small coffee table at his side as the dog, still growling, went by him.

'Get back in your box Lady,' he snapped as he swiped at her with the book, catching the dog a sharp blow on her back. She gave a yelp and lay in submission on the carpet.

'She's okay, Alan,' smiled Laxton, softening the tone of his voice as he reached out with his hand.

The dog gave a submissive whine, before rolling over on her back and allowing him to stroke her belly, her eyes were half closed as she lapped up the attention she was receiving. She was suddenly brought back to reality as a sharp voice said, 'Lady! Get back in that box.'

It was Alan's mum Marie. She had just entered the room carrying a tray with the three mugs of coffee on it. The dog sprang to her feet and in two seconds was back in her box.

The inspector, an appreciative smile on his face, thanked her before reaching out and picking up one of the mugs.

'Do you think our Alan will make out in his new job Inspector?'

'Aw Mum,' spluttered the red-faced young man, who had just taken a sip of his coffee.

Laxton grinned mischievously as he told her, 'He'll do.'

Another twenty minutes of exchanging pleasantries went by before Laxton checked his watch.

'Half past five,' he mumbled, half to himself. 'It's time I was off.'

'So soon?' Marie put to him, a little disappointedly.

'We've got a busy day in front of us tomorrow,' he told her as he pushed himself to his feet and prepared to leave.

'What time do you reckon you will be here in the morning?' enquired his young partner as they approached the front door.

'Mmm,' muttered Laxton. 'I would say about nine o'clock.'

Thanking Marie again for her hospitality, he walked out of the door and strode purposefully to his car. He had a smile of contentment on his face as he waved to Alan and his mother before accelerating away.

'Quite a man your Mr Laxton, Alan,' she muttered,

a warm smile on her flushed face as she closed the door.

Laxton hummed to the music emanating from the car radio as he exited Wragby and drove the twenty-five miles or so to his cottage in Old Bolingbroke. Darkness was just beginning to close in as he turned into his driveway. Annie was in the act of placing his dinner of lamb chops in the oven to keep warm as he walked into the kitchen.

'Something smells really good Annie,' he told her as he took his coat off and hung it on the back of a chair. Horatio was weaving in and out of his feet, purring away as Laxton pulled out the chair from under the table and sat down. A few minutes later Annie placed the steaming hot meal in front of him.

'There you are Mr Laxton,' she said as she stood back.

'Annie you are a gem,' he muttered appreciatively as he reached out and squeezed her arm affectionately.

'Get away with you!' she exclaimed, her round face beaming as she pulled on her coat in readiness to leave.

Annie had been what you might call his 'carer' for more than ten years and had become very precious to him.

'I'll see you in the morning,' she called out to him as she went through the door and climbed on her bike.

Laxton, his mouth full, raised his hand in reply before returning to the somewhat satisfying chore of eating the appetising meal that she had placed in front of him. An hour later, after taking a shower he stretched out on the settee, a whisky and soda in his hand as he enjoyed the haunting music of Johann Strauss and his 'Tales from the Vienna woods'.

Chapter 8

The sound of a cuckoo could be heard greeting the morning sun which was just showing above the hills that surrounded Old Bolingbroke as Laxton climbed into his car and drove it out of the driveway and on to the narrow country lane that ran through the quiet village. A heavy morning mist hung over the remains of the castle and the surrounding countryside as he carefully made his way out of the village, the mist dissipating as he climbed the hill that led to the main road. Half an hour later after negotiating Horncastle and Baumber, he arrived at Wragby; he checked his watch; it showed eight fifty. Grunting his approval he made his way to his young partner's home. A smartly dressed Alan was waiting at the gate of the semi-detached house as he braked to a stop; jumping in the car the young man nodded good morning to the inspector before fastening his seatbelt. His mum Marie who was standing in the doorway waved them off.

'Now then Alan,' began Laxton as he selected a higher gear and accelerated. 'We'll stop off at headquarters and check what the chief has for us.'

Half an hour or so later, after being held up by the slower heavy traffic, they eventually arrived at headquarters and parked up; the two officers climbed out of the car and made their way to the double glass door entrance. Laxton smiled as he saw a little old lady giving a red faced Bellows a telling off as they approached the chief's office; after a slight tap on the door they walked in.

Wilberton, sitting back with his arms folded, had a serious expression on his face as the two officers entered the room.

'Good morning Chief,' declared Laxton and Billings in unison.

Wilberton acknowledged them with a slight wave of his hand as the two men took a seat in front of him. Looking over the rims of his glasses he addressed the inspector.

'I've just received a call from the bank manager. It seems he is expecting some vital information regarding the cheques that we have been looking in to,' he intoned, a serious expression on his face. 'I want you to go to the bank and see what you can glean from him.'

Laxton nodded his head.

'We'll get on to it right away,' he declared as he prepared to get to his feet.

The young man nodded his head in agreement before following the inspector through the door.

The two men gave Bellows a wave as they pushed open the glass door and walked across the car park to the car. Laxton handed the car keys to Billings telling him, 'You drive Alan, I've got some thinking to do.'

After they had got in the car, Billings, with his serious looking senior at his side, guided the car out of the car park and on to the road. The traffic was getting heavy in the centre of Lincoln as they approached the bank. A few minutes later after parking the car they entered the bank. A smiling John Mulbeck greeted them with a handshake before leading them into his office.

'Now er, Mr Laxton isn't it?' he said, his query directed at the older man as the two police officers took their seats in front of him.

The inspector nodded his head at the bank manager, a slight smile on his face as he clasped his hands in his lap.

'First of all,' he declared, somewhat officiously. 'I must tell you that the little information that I have been able to come up with from the tabs up to the present time isn't going to get us far.'

Laxton, his brow furrowed, leaned forward in his seat and addressed Mulbeck. 'I think we should be the judge of that sir,' he told the red-haired man, somewhat sharply, causing Mulbeck's face to match his hair.

'Hrumph!' he exclaimed uncomfortably. 'You may be right Inspector.'

Following this exchange he reached forward, opened a drawer in his desk and took out a sheet of paper.

Placing it on the top of his desk he took out his glasses and sat for a few seconds perusing it before telling them, 'What I have here is the name of the person, who has cashed one of the cheques in this country.'

'What about the others?' enquired Billings.

Mulbeck looked at the young man over the thick rims of his glasses. 'If I had discovered those I would have said so,' he almost whispered through thin lips.

Laxton turned to Billings, a disapproving expression on his face. His young partner shrugged his shoulder and retreated back into his seat.

'As I was saying,' went on Mulbeck. 'We have only got the name but at the moment no address.'

'May I see the information that you've received?' requested Laxton.

'Yes by all means!' exclaimed the manager, handing over the sheet of paper.

The inspector nodded his thanks, as he took the paper containing the name of the person who had cashed the cheque, from him. There wasn't much in the way of detailed information written on the form he told himself as he took out his glasses and ran his eyes over it. It stated that the name of the person who had cashed one of the cheques was one, M. Fulbek. And that it had been cashed in the National Bank in Boston. Laxton took his glasses off and chewed on one of the ear rests for a few seconds before coming to a decision. He turned to his partner.

'Alan, I think we should go to Boston and have a word with the bank manager,' he said firmly.

Turning to Mulbeck he thanked him for his help and handed him the sheet of paper.

Mulbeck raised his hands. 'You keep it!' he exclaimed.

Laxton thanked him as he placed the paper in his pocket and got to his feet, then, after shaking hands with him, the two officers exited the bank and made their way to the car. After climbing in the passenger seat and fastening his seatbelt, he turned to Billings and told him, 'Right Alan, when you are ready, we'll make our way to Boston.'

The young man nodded his head before engaging the gears, driving out of the car park and negotiating the busy Lincoln centre. Laxton was deep in thought as they joined the main highway.

Fifty minutes later they were entering the ancient city of Boston overlooked by the towering St. Botolphs, known locally as Boston Stump. Billings parked up before he and the inspector walked across the busy town centre to where Lloyds' offices were situated. The manager, James Barley who had been informed by Mulbeck that they were coming to see him greeted them with a friendly smile as he shook their hands and led them to his office where they introduced themselves before taking a seat.

'Now then gentlemen!' he exclaimed, leaning his elbows on the desk in front of him. 'How can I help you?'

Laxton clasped his hands in his lap before looking the smartly dressed forty-year-old in the eyes and informing him that they were investigating the person who had cashed the cheque in his bank.

'In what way can I help?' enquired the bank manager, a questioning frown on his forehead.

Laxton explained to him that they were looking into the whereabouts of the person whose name was M. Fulbek.

Barley, deep in thought, mulled over in his mind what the inspector had told him, before enquiring, 'What exactly did you have in mind?'

Laxton paused for a couple of seconds before replying to the manager's query.

'First of all can you give us the date when the cheque was cashed?'

The manager pushed his seat back and pulled open a drawer in his desk; delving into it, he spent a few seconds shuffling through numerous sheets of paper.

'Here we are,' he declared as he drew one of the sheets of paper out and ran his eyes over it. 'It states here that the cheque was drawn on May the fifth nineteen sixty-nine.'

At that moment Billings spoke up. 'Would it be possible for you to tell us this person's address sir?'

His senior partner compressed his lips in annoyance at the interruption but said nothing. Barley gave a half smile before telling them that would not be possible.

'The only path that I can advise you to take is to check the name in the phone book.'

'Do you have a phone book handy?' enquired the inspector.

'Yes,' replied Barley, reaching down behind his desk and pulling open a drawer.

'There you are, be my guest,' he declared as he dropped the heavy phone book on the desk.

Laxton nodded his thanks as he got to his feet and picked up the thick book. After scanning carefully through the pages; running his finger down the long list, he suddenly stopped and gave a satisfied grunt.

'Here we are!' he exclaimed. 'M. Fulbek, Dyke Cottage, East Lane, Skeldyke. Lincs.'

'Ah yes I know the place,' declared the manager.

'It's about eight miles outside Boston, just off the A16.'

After thanking him for his help the two officers made their way out of the bank and to the car.

Laxton, once again, sat in the passenger seat. He pulled out a map, took out his reading glasses and put them on before running his eyes over it.

'Here we are,' he declared, placing his forefinger on a place on the map; as the manager had told them, it was just off the A16.

A few minutes later they were wending their way through the busy streets of Boston, eventually coming to a roundabout on the outskirts of the town. A sign indicated the A16 to Spalding.

The inspector nodded his head in approval as Billings drove on to the roundabout and took that route. Fifteen minutes later he turned off the main highway when he saw a sign with an arrow pointing to Skeldyke. After what was a pleasant drive through the open countryside they eventually arrived at the village in question.

'Take your time now Alan,' advised Laxton as they approached the small village with a row of cottages on either side of the lane that ran through it. They all had long front gardens.

The young man nodded his head and slowed to about ten miles an hour as the inspector carefully scrutinised each property. They had come to the last one on their left when Laxton gripped his arm.

'Hold it Alan,' he blurted out loud. 'I think this is it.'

Billings put his foot on the brake and stopped the car.

The property in question was an old cottage with

ivy covering the front wall, almost obscuring the small windows. Hung over the porch was a sign with 'Dyke Cottage', written on it.

The two men climbed out of the car, pushed open the rickety gate that was hanging on one hinge, and made their way along the crazy paved footpath to the heavy wooden door.

'Must be two hundred years old!' exclaimed Billings in a low voice as he reached up and lifted the cast iron doorknocker. There was a loud barking and growling as he gave two sharp raps on it, then stood back and waited for someone to answer. After a few seconds the sound of shoes clip-clopping their way to the door and the key being turned in the lock, could be heard. The door half opened and a woman's face peered round the edge of it.

'Can I help you?' she said a little breathlessly as she struggled to hold back the black Labrador.

'We are making enquiries about an M. Fulbek,' Laxton put to the forty-year-old buxom blonde.

Still holding on to the dog she looked up at the two men. 'And who might you be?' she demanded, nastily.

'Er, I'm sorry we haven't introduced ourselves,' he stammered, a little apologetically, before going on to tell her that they were policemen.

'Oh well!' she exclaimed. 'Why didn't you say so in the first place?'

There was a distinct softening to the tone of her voice as she invited them in.

Thanking her they followed her into the small back kitchen. There was a strong smell of damp as they waited for her to take the dog outside and fasten it up.

'Now then, what do you want to know?' she asked them, fastening her long hair back in a ponytail, as she came back into the kitchen.

Laxton paused for a moment, stroking his chin as he looked down into the blue eyes of the woman in front of him.

'First of all, is your name Fulbek?' he put to her in a quiet tone of voice.

'No it isn't,' she replied, reaching up and scratching at what looked like a wart on the side of her rather long nose before going on to tell him: 'My name is Lumley, er, Marjory Lumley.'

'Can you prove that?' asked Laxton, a serious expression on his face.

The woman straightened up, her eyes slits.

'Are you calling me a liar Inspector?' she retorted sharply.

Laxton, held his hands up; there was a smile on his face as he attempted to appease the indignant woman.

'No, no, I can assure you I have good reasons for asking.'

It was obvious to him that she wasn't the person they were looking for. He tried another tack.

'If, as you say your name is not Fulbek,' he put to her. 'Is it possible that you may have heard the name?'

'Not really,' she replied with a slight shake of her head before telling him: 'We've only been living here about ten months.'

At that moment there was a bang as the back door slammed shut.

'That will be my husband, Albert,' she confided. Lowering her voice she added, 'Noisy sod.'

At that moment a tall, gaunt, scruffy looking man in his fifties walked through the door, took off his cap exposing his balding head before hanging the cap on a hook in the back of what looked to be a clothes closet under the stairs; he turned and directed his attention to the two strangers.

'What's going on here then?' he enquired sharply.

'It's the police Al,' his wife explained.

Laxton introduced himself and his partner. Lumley visibly relaxed as he nodded his head and shook their hands.

'What can we do for you?' queried the thin man.

'We are enquiring about someone named M. Fulbek.' He stopped for a moment as he coughed and cleared his throat before going on. 'We were led to believe that the person was residing at this address.'

There was a rasping sound as Lumley ran the palm of his hand over his unshaven chin; his eyes were half closed as he thought over what the inspector had said.

'I've explained to them that we've only been here about ten months,' his wife said, butting in.

'That's true,' he remarked with a nod of his head before going on to tell them: 'The tenants before us were named Johnston.'

'Would your neighbours be able to help us?' enquired Billings, looking up from the notebook that he held in his hand, on which he had been diligently taking notes.

'The best one to contact would be Mrs Goldworthy, she's been around here for donkey's years. She's a nosey old bugger and doesn't miss much,' he chuckled, displaying discoloured teeth as he did so.

'Where does she live?' enquired the inspector.

'Across the lane, second cottage down,' replied Lumley.

After thanking the couple for their help the two officers left and made their way across the lane to the white-washed cottage that had been indicated. There was a movement of curtains as they approached the front gate of the appropriately named 'White Cottage'. A few seconds later they lifted the cast-iron knocker and rapped on the heavy wooden door. A few seconds later the door could be heard being unlocked followed by the sound of two heavy bolts being drawn back. Laxton repressed a smile as he muttered under his breath.

'It's like Fort Knox.'

Eventually the heavy door slowly opened. The grey head of an elderly lady who looked to about four foot ten, poked round the edge of it. A pair of rheumy blue eyes looked up at the two tall men.

'Can I help you?' enquired a quavering voice.

Billings stepped forward and explained to the old lady as gently as he could, that they were the police and that they were making enquiries about one of her neighbours. After a quick glance up and down the lane she asked them, 'Won't you come in?'

The two officers stepped into the old fashioned, papered hallway and stood by as she closed the door; a few seconds later she led them into the front room, telling them with a smile, 'It's more comfy in here.'

The two men nodded their thanks and sat down on the soft well-worn settee.

'I'll make you a nice cup of tea,' she told them, disappearing into the kitchen before they could say no.

Laxton sat quietly, his hands clasped in front of him. His partner had his pen and a writing pad at the ready as they cast their eyes round the lived in room. There were numerous oil paintings hung on the walls. Laxton studied them intently before the old lady came in carrying a tray with three cups, a teapot and all the necessary utensils on it; there was also a plate with the biscuits on it.

'Now then gentlemen,' she said a little sharply, as she poured out the teas. 'If you want sugar and milk, you can get it yourselves.'

Laxton smiled inwardly at the somewhat bossy attitude of the little woman. He nodded his head as she sat down and almost disappeared behind the large coffee table. After putting sugar and milk in his tea he turned to her as he stirred it with the spoon provided.

'Mrs Goldworthy isn't it?' he put to her before taking a sip of his tea.

'It is,' she replied with a nod of her grey head at the inspector, her rheumy blue eyes twinkling.

'What is it you want to know?'

'First of all Mrs Goldworthy…'

She held her hand up, stopping him mid-sentence.

'Call me Anne,' she told him, looking up into his grey eyes.

'Okay,' he rejoined. 'Anne it is.' Then he went on. 'As I was saying Anne, what I want to know is have you heard the name, Fulbek?'

The little woman studied what he had said for a few seconds before telling him, 'Yes, Mr and Mrs Fulbek, they lived across the lane at Dyke Cottage.'

She paused for a moment before going on to tell

them, 'She did say that his first name was, Martin.'

Laxton, a serious expression on his face, looked across at his partner who was ready with his pen and pad, before turning to the old lady and asking her, 'Did you know them intimately?'

Anne shrugged her shoulders, telling him, 'None of the neighbours got to know them really well. She and her partner always kept to themselves.'

Billings leaned forward and asked her, 'Did they live there long?'

'Not really,' she rejoined with a shake of her grey head. 'I would say they were living there for just over a year.'

'When did they leave?' he persisted.

She half closed her eyes for a few seconds. Billings looked across at Laxton, wondering if she had gone to sleep. Suddenly she opened them.

'Now let me see,' she muttered as she counted on her fingers. 'Before the Lumleys there were a couple named Johnston, who were there for about nine years. Before them there were the Marston's; they were there for around five years. I would say it was around fifteen years ago,' she told him, adding, 'just before my husband Alec died. Bless him.'

'Did they have any children?' enquired the inspector, leaning forward in his seat.

'Not while they were here,' she rejoined with a shake of her head.

'So they had no children?' Billings put in questioningly.

'I didn't say that,' she told him a little sharply, before going on to tell them that they had four children with them when they took up residence at the cottage. 'There was one thing that I could never understand,' she muttered almost to herself.

'What would that be?' enquired Laxton.

'The fact that they were all around the same age, and that they were obviously not twins or quads,' was her reply.

'What do you mean by the same age?' enquired Billings, sucking the end of the biro.

'Well they were all such small things. I would say that they were either three or four years old.'

She plucked at her wrinkled bottom lip for a few seconds before carrying on.

'Alec always said that they were fostered.'

'Oh and what made him think that?' Billings put to her.

'Well, I would say that within nine months of them getting here the children had all gone,' she replied with a shrug of her frail shoulders.

What do you mean by 'gone'?' interjected the inspector. 'Did they all go at once?'

Anne shook her grey head vigorously.

'No! No!' she exclaimed sharply. 'The children went over a period of around six months.'

'You said that the Fulbeks lived there for about a year. Did they ever mention where they were moving to?'

'There were odd times when I got talking to her she kept on about friends that she'd got in a village named Frithville, that's on the other side of Boston.' She paused for a moment before adding almost as an afterthought, 'Er that's in Lincolnshire you know.'

'Did she mention an address?' enquired Billings, his pen poised over his notebook.

The old lady's wrinkled face broke into a half smile as she looked into the young man's eyes and told him with a slight shake of her head, 'I'm afraid she didn't tell me the address.'

Laxton, who had been listening intently to the exchanges, sat with his hands clasped in front of him for a few moments deep in thought; suddenly he straightened up pressed his hands against his knees and got to his feet.

'I think that will do us for now Alan,' he announced firmly.

After thanking the old lady for her help, they walked out of the cottage and into the warm sunshine. He stopped halfway up the garden path and cast his eyes around the numerous flowers that were beginning to bloom.

'Beautiful,' he muttered with a slight shake of his head as he drank in the scene, before following Billings to the car.

Ten minutes later they left the sleepy village behind and joined the traffic on the A16 that would take them through Boston on their way back to Lincoln.

Laxton sat back in the passenger seat deep in contemplation, before turning to his young partner.

'What do you think then Alan?' he put to him.

Alan gave a shrug of his shoulders.

'Very interesting, but we don't seem to have made a lot of progress.'

Laxton smiled at Billings' summing up.

'I wouldn't say that,' he rejoined with a slight shake of his head.

Billings took a quick glance across at him as a sign indicating 'Frithville 6 miles', flashed past.

'Shouldn't we be going there?' he put to the inspector a little urgently.

Laxton, who had also seen the sign, shook his head.

'We need to know a good bit more about the situation before we go dashing around the countryside willy-nilly.'

'What's our next move then?'

'Well after we've seen the chief at headquarters and talked over our progress so far and collated all information regarding the case, then we will make a positive move.'

He stopped for a moment and checked his watch. It showed twelve thirty.

'On second thoughts I reckon it would be a good idea to stop somewhere and have a meal,' he muttered, adding, 'I know just the place.'

Thirty minutes later upon his instructions, they turned off the busy main road and drew into the parking area of the 'The Red Lion' in Partney, which was ironically directly opposite the local church. *An ideal situation, one for commiseration the other for celebration*, thought Laxton as they climbed out of the car and made their way through the rear glass door which led to the bar. Laxton nodded his head at the barman, 'Nigel' who incidentally was also the owner. The inspector had called in for a meal on numerous occasions over the years.

'Now then gents what will you have?' he enquired,

a pleasant smile on his face.

'We'll have two half glasses of bitter shandy and two portions of haddock and chips,' the inspector told him.

After picking up the two drinks the two officers were directed to a large dining room by 'Christine' who took their orders. Taking a seat Laxton leaned back and took a long satisfying drink. He crossed his arms and ran his eyes over the paintings of what looked like numerous battles during the Napoleonic wars.

'We'll get a good meal here,' he whispered to his young partner. 'I've dropped in here in the past and it had always been an enjoyable experience.'

At that moment a young woman approached the table; the two men sat back as she laid out the necessary utensils.

'It will only be a few minutes,' she told them a broad smile on her pretty face as she turned away.

Alan nodded his head and smiled back.

Eventually Christine placed two trays on the table. A few minutes later she arrived with the appetising meal.

'There you are gentlemen,' she declared as she placed the large oval plates in front of them. 'Enjoy your meal.'

Laxton thanked her with a nod of his head and a smile, before rubbing the palms of his hands together as he contemplated the huge haddock and the heap of chips that had been placed in front of each of them.

Alan had only one word to say before tucking in: 'Wow!'

Fifteen minutes later two very satisfied customers

leaned back in their chairs and patted their stomachs.

'That was really something,' the young man declared as Christine approached them.

'Was everything okay gents?' she enquired.

Laxton took a deep breath and loosened his belt another notch. 'Spot on,' he remarked as he took out his wallet.

'I'll pay for my own meal,' blurted out Billings, standing up and reaching into his pocket as he did so.

The inspector held out his hand, assuring him with a firm, 'It's on me Alan.'

A reluctant, red-faced Billings sat down and finished off his drink. Laxton followed suit before getting to his feet.

'Right, we'll be on our way!' he exclaimed a little sharply.

After once again thanking the staff for an extremely enjoyable meal, the two officers exited the pub. Laxton glanced up at the sky as they walked across the car park. It didn't look too promising, he thought to himself as they climbed in the car. A few minutes later, with Billings driving, they were making their way back to headquarters in Lincoln.

'What do you think of the way things are going so far Inspector?' he enquired, casting a sideways glance at his superior.

Laxton sat back in his seat for a few seconds, deep in thought, before answering.

'It looks to me as though this Martin Fulbek moved to a different area after the children had gone, possibly in order to cover his or their tracks.'

He paused for a moment as he pressed his

clenched fist against his chin before saying, 'The problem is where did they move to next, almost ten years ago?'

He gave a shrug of his shoulders, a look of frustration on his face as he added, 'They could be anywhere.'

Heavy, black clouds hung over the Three Sisters, threatening to envelope them as the two detectives approached the outskirts of Lincoln. Large spots of rains were beginning to fall as they pulled into the headquarters car park. Jumping out of the car they made a rush for the entrance. Pushing open the heavy glass door they burst a little breathlessly into the reception.

Sergeant Bellows who was sat at a desk making out some paperwork, glanced up at the red faced pair as they made their entry, greeting them with a smile as they walked through the door

The inspector nodded his head in response, before approaching the chief's office and knocking on the door.

'Come in,' called out Chief Inspector Wilberton. 'Ahh Robert!' he exclaimed, getting to his feet, as the two tall detectives walked through the door and approached his desk. 'What have you come up with?'

Laxton drew up one of the two seats that stood against the office wall and sat down. Billings took the other one.

'Sergeant,' called out the chief in a loud voice.

Bellows stuck his head round the door.

'Yes Chief,' he replied sharply.

'Send three coffees in will you?' he requested before turning his attention to the inspector.

'Now then, what have we got?'

Laxton went over all the details that they had gleaned so far regarding the missing children, who by now would be young adults around twenty years old.

Wilberton sat back his arms folded as he contemplated the information that the inspector had come up with. 'It seems to me that the facts show that they had the four children with them in 1968, which was the same year that the families that we have been in contact with lost their children.'

He pressed his forefinger against his lips as he cast his mind back to that unfortunate period when the police could not find any clues as to where they were.

'As things are at the moment we know that one of the children that the Fulbeks had abducted was Elizabeth Watling, now known as Rebecca Malling. She's twenty years old. That means that the other three children that they had would also be nineteen or twenty years old.'

At that moment a young, pretty WPC, her long blonde hair tied in a bun at the back of her head came in the room carrying a tray with three mugs of coffee on it. She cast a glance out of the corner of her blue eyes at Alan as she leaned across him and placed the tray on the desk; the young detective gave her a half smile as she drew back and walked out of the room leaving a strong smell of perfume behind her.

'Harrumph!' exclaimed the chief in an attempt to attract Billings, whose eyes had been following the shapely young woman.

He had a stern expression on his face as he turned to the business in hand.

'When you are ready Constable,' he snapped.

Billings, his face reddening, gave his undivided attention as the chief went on. 'The one good thing that we do know is that the children are all probably alive,' he told them, adding in a low voice: 'That wasn't the case at the time they went missing.'

Laxton leaned forward in his chair, his hands clasped in front of him as he asked the chief, 'Have we had any further contact with the bank?'

'No I'm afraid not,' the chief replied with a shake of his head. 'They did say that they would contact us if anything came up. Did you come up with any information regarding their present whereabouts?'

'Mrs Goldworthy did inform us that the Fulbeks were talking about friends they had in a village named Frithville.'

The chief scratched the back of his head for a few seconds. 'They do seem to have been keeping on the move,' he muttered.

'That could be deliberate Chief, it could be a ploy to cover their tracks,' suggested Billings.

'You are probably right Constable,' the chief rejoined somewhat sombrely. 'The problem is, up to now they seem to have made quite a good fist of it.'

At that moment Bellows pushed his head round the door.

'Chief!' he exclaimed. 'The bank manager is on the phone.'

Wilberton's eyes lit up.

'Put him through Sergeant,' he rejoined as he put his coffee down, reached out for the telephone on his desk and put it to his ear.

'Yes, yes I've got that,' he muttered into the

mouthpiece. After nodding his head a couple of times he put the phone down and gazed at his fingers with which he had formed a pyramid.

'The manager tells me that the other three cheques has been cashed around the same time as the first one by the Fulbeks,' he told the two detectives.

'Did he say where?' enquired Laxton, his brow furrowed.

The chief paused for a moment and looked the inspector in the eyes.

'He says that they were cashed in Boston in August sixty-nine.' He paused for a moment, his brow creased in concentration before adding, 'That would make it around three months after the first one.'

'I reckon that must have been just after he moved away from Skeldyke,' interjected Laxton as he tipped his mug and drank the rest of his coffee, before getting to his feet and checking his watch, it showed three forty-five.

'Mmm, there isn't much more we can achieve today,' he muttered as he turned to leave.

Billings dutifully got to his feet ready to follow him.

'Robert, you said that the old lady told you that the Fulbeks had friends in Frithville,' Wilberton stated as the inspector turned to leave.

Laxton nodded his head in agreement, telling him, 'Yes that's true. The problem is they told her that some years ago.' He gave a shrug of his shoulders as he told Wilberton, 'We'll sort something out tomorrow Chief.'

With this, the two detectives walked out of the room and with a wave to Bellows, they made their way to the car. A few spots of rain were beginning to fall as Laxton climbed into the driver's seat. A few seconds later after Billings had settled down, he pulled out of the car park and set off on the journey home, twenty minutes later they arrived at Wragby.

'Here we are Alan,' declared the inspector, stopping the car outside the front gate.

Alan's mum, a broad smile on her face, was peering through the window and giving a wave of her hand as he thanked the inspector, before jumping out of the car and making a dash through the rain, for the door. After a smile and a wave of his hand in return Laxton set off on the rest of his journey home. He had plenty to occupy his mind as he turned off the main road and drove along the winding lane that led into Old Bolingbroke.

The rain had stopped and the sun which was low in the sky was beginning to dip down over the tree tops, as he arrived at his cottage; turning into the driveway, he stopped the car and climbed out. Horatio was meowing as he weaved in and out of his master's feet, almost tripping him up. Laxton bent down and picked the ginger cat up, placed him on his shoulder and stroked him affectionately as he made his way into the cottage.

'You are early Mister Laxton,' a woman's voice called out from the kitchen as he closed the door behind him and made his entrance. It was his housekeeper Annie.

'Yes,' he replied. 'It's a very rare occasion.'

Annie, who was making pastry, looked round at him as he walked into the kitchen; she had a disapproving expression on her flour-smudged face when she saw Horatio on his shoulder, telling him, 'I don't like that cat in the kitchen when I'm cooking.'

'Sorry Horatio, it looks as though you've got the order of the boot,' he quipped as he placed the cat on the floor outside the kitchen door, before closing it and going over to the short bonnie woman, placing his hands on her shoulders and whispering in her ear: 'What's on the menu today, Annie my dear?'

'I'm going to bake you a meat and potato pie,' she told him, giggling as she wriggled out of his hands and carried the rolled out pastry and laid it out carefully on a dish of meat and veg that stood further along the worktop.

'My favourite dish,' he muttered, his mouth watering at the thought of it.

'If you go upstairs and get your shower it will be about ready when you come back down,' she told him in a tone of voice that made it sound more of an order.

He stood up to attention in front of her and executed a perfect salute.

'Yes sir,' he replied snappily, a half-grin on his face.

'Get away with you, you soft thing,' she declared, a broad smile on her face as she took in his boyish antics.

Without any more ado, he turned, walked out of the kitchen and up the stairs, telling her, 'I'll get my shower.'

Half an hour or so later he came back down wearing a dressing gown. There was a very appetising aroma coming from the kitchen as he strode into the kitchen to be met by the broad rump of his housekeeper as she bent down to take the pie out of the oven.

'Annie that pie smells really good,' he enthused as he sat at the table and poured himself a can of Guinness.

After taking a good swallow of the inviting, dark, frothy drink, he sat back as Annie placed a steaming hot portion of meat and potato pie in front of him. She smiled as he picked up his knife and fork with a, 'My dear I'm going to really enjoy this,' before tucking in with gusto.

'I'll be off now Mister Laxton,' she told him as she pulled on her coat.

His mouth being full, he nodded his head, raised his hand and mumbled his thanks as she walked out of the door.

Ten minutes later he was patting his stomach and finishing what remained of his drink, before stretching out on the settee and making himself comfortable as he went over the day's events to the relaxing strains of Johann Strauss in the background.

Chapter 9

Martin Fulbek, a big, heavily built six-footer in his mid-fifties, was deep in thought as he pulled into the driveway and switched off the engine. He ran his big hands over his close-cropped greying hair as he sat for a couple of minutes contemplating the significance of the information he had received.

'Dammit,' he growled, smashing his right fist into the palm of his left hand before taking a deep breath and climbing out of his car and making his way along the path that ran alongside the front garden to the front door.

'You don't seem to be in a very good mood!' a woman's voice exclaimed when the door banged shut. It was his partner Janet, preparing a meal. She looked round as he entered the kitchen, he had a worried expression on his face as he pulled a dining chair out from under the table and sat down.

'What's the matter?' she enquired in a low voice.

He stroked his chin for a few seconds before telling her in an ominous tone, 'Janet, they may be on to us.'

Her face went white as she sat down and brushed back her long dark tresses that had fallen over her brown eyes.

'Who may be on to us?' she put to him, her voice strained.

He paused for a moment to gather his thoughts before going on to tell her, 'I bumped into one of our neighbours from Skeldyke; he told me that the police have been asking questions about the children,'

'But it was so long ago, how could they…?'

He raised his hand as he butted in on her.

'I've been making some discreet enquiries and I have discovered that one of the couples we dealt with was recently involved in an accident on the motorway.'

He chewed on his lip nervously as he let the information sink in before continuing.

'The girl that we placed with them uncovered evidence pointing to the fact that she had been adopted.'

He gave shrug of his broad shoulders as he went on to tell her that the girl, who was now twenty, had gone to the police.

'Which one of the children was it?'

'The first one that we let go, Elizabeth Watling,' he told her.

'The couple we let her go to was named Malling if I remember rightly,' muttered Janet, her eyes half closed as she cast her mind back.

Martin Fulbek nodded his head in agreement before telling her, his voice taking on a note of gravity, 'They were both killed in the car accident,'

Janet put her hand to her mouth, her brow deeply furrowed as she absorbed the information.

'When exactly did this happen?' she almost whispered.

'I'm not quite sure of the exact date,' he rejoined with a shake of his head.

'Does this mean we will have to move away from here and find somewhere else to live?'

He paused for a moment, deep in thought as he stroked his chin.

'It looks that way,' he told her, looking deep into her eyes.

'How long have we got?'

He thought over what she had said for a few seconds before telling her, 'Not long Janet. It seems that the police have been making enquiries around Skeldyke and one of the neighbours told them that we had moved to the Frithville area.'

'What do you reckon we should do?' she asked him shakily.

'Don't worry I'll set something up for us in readiness to leave in the next couple of days.'

Suddenly her head dropped into her hands as she sobbed uncontrollably.

'Why did we agree to take in those children Martin?' she questioned, looking up at him through tear-filled eyes. 'We'll never be able to settle anywhere. We will always be on the run.'

He placed a consoling hand on the back of her bowed head.

'We will have to get in touch with the rest of the

group and ask them, for their help,' he declared, adding, 'they've had their share of the money.'

He went over to the phone, picked it up and dialled a number. A few seconds later he spoke into the mouthpiece and asked for a Mister Wooding. Another few seconds went by then he straightened up.

'Hello,' he said a little sharply into the phone. 'Is that Thomas?'

The next few minutes were taken up with him describing the situation that they had found themselves in. After a few nods of his head he slowly put the phone down.

'What did he say?' she asked him, a note of urgency in her voice

He turned and looked down at her. 'He's told me that we have to sit tight for a couple of days until they find us alternative accommodation.'

She looked up at him, questioningly. 'That doesn't leave us much time to prepare,'

'I agree,' he muttered before telling her somewhat secretively, 'I don't want you to mention anything to the neighbours about us moving,'

She shook her head from side to side.

'I won't,' she promised him.

The rest of the day dragged as they worried about getting a call from the police. They knew that if they were caught it could mean years in prison.

The following morning at ten o'clock the phone rang; Martin Fulbek picked it up and put it to his ear.

'Hello,' he said gruffly. After a few seconds of nodding his head at the receiver, he put it down. There was a serious expression on his face as he turned to Janet. 'We leave as soon as we can,' he told her solemnly.

'Where are we going?'

He held his hand up.

'I'll tell you when we leave,' he informed her, adding: 'In the meantime we'll get what we can in the car in readiness.'

Robert Laxton was humming to himself as he drove through the relaxing countryside on his way to Lincoln. It was a lovely morning and he was feeling good.

After twenty minutes or so he drew up outside the front gate of his young partner's home. DC Alan Billings was ready and waiting as he stopped the car; the young man gave a quick wave and a smile to his mother as he strode up the path before climbing in the car and joining his superior. Laxton also returned the wave as his young partner fastened his seatbelt, before accelerating away.

'What's on the agenda today?' enquired the young man as he settled back in his seat.

'It will depend on what information the chief's got for us,' declared Laxton as he pulled out to overtake a couple of elderly cyclists before joining the heavy traffic on the main road.

The rest of the journey was completed in silence as the inspector concentrated on his driving.

Twenty minutes later they arrived at headquarters. Bellows greeted them with a nod of his head as they entered the building and made their way across the reception area and gave a knock on the chief's door.

Wilberton looked up from the sheet of paper that he was studying as they entered his office. His brow was furrowed as he leaned back in his chair; taking off his glasses he addressed the two officers as they each took a seat in front of him.

'I've just received information that the Fulbeks may be residing at this address,' he told them, pushing the sheet of paper towards the inspector.

Laxton reached out, picked it up and studied it for a few seconds.

'Mmm North Cottage, Frithville,' he muttered before looking up at Wilberton and reminding him that was the area that the old lady had mentioned.

The chief nodded his head in agreement.

'Yes it turned out to be a good lead,' he rejoined before going on to inform them that he had got in touch with Boston council and they had informed him that a couple named Fulbek lived in Frithville at that address.

Wilberton sat back in his chair his hands clasped in front of him as he addressed the inspector. 'Robert I want you to go to this address in Frithville immediately and see what you can come up with.'

'Okay Chief, we'll get down there right away,' declared Laxton as he got to his feet and turned to leave followed closely by Billings.

The sun was shining down from a cloudless sky as they made their way to the car. Laxton tossed the keys to his partner with a, 'You drive Alan.'

A few minutes later they were on their way. Laxton leaned back and relaxed as they sped along the busy highway, the warmth of the sun almost putting him to sleep as they neared Boston. A sign pointing to

Frithville came up on their right. Billings slowed down and followed the sign. Fifteen minutes later they were approaching the village. A sign with Frithville on it told them that they had arrived. Billings drove slowly through the small village as Laxton checked the names as they passed the scattered cottages.

'Here we are!' he exclaimed, a little abruptly.

Billings stopped the car on the front of the property. A car with its boot lid up stood in the driveway in front of the adjoining garage as they climbed out and walked down the path that ran along the side of a long garden, Laxton had a look of distaste on his face as he took in the uncut lawn and the numerous weeds that were sprouting up among the flowers that were growing along the borders of it; Billings reached up, lifted the brass knocker and rapped on the heavy wooden door.

Martin Fulbek had just finished placing almost all the necessary possessions in the car that they would need in the days and weeks to come; the only exception being a case which they were about to take with them.

'That should do us,' he stated with a note of satisfaction as he walked into the lounge and joined Janet.

'What time are we leaving Martin?'

He looked at his watch before telling her, 'In about five minutes.'

At that moment a car drew up on the lane at the front of the cottage. Two tall men climbed out.

'A car has just stopped on the front Martin,'

gasped Janet, her hand covering her mouth as she muttered, 'it might be the police.'

The big man looked through the window and saw two men striding down the path. There was a sharp rap on the door.

'You answer it Janet,' he ordered harshly.

'What shall I tell them?'

'Never mind, just answer it,' he snapped, pushing her towards the door.

Slowly opening the door she looked up at the two men standing there.

Laxton looked down at the woman who had answered the door.

'Yes,' she said somewhat nervously.

'We are the police, am I speaking to Mrs Fulbek?' stated the inspector.

'Yes that's me,' she informed him, nodding her head.

'We are making a few enquiries,' he told her, adding, 'may we come in?'

At that moment a big hard man came to the door, roughly pushed past the woman and almost knocked the inspector over as he rammed his way past them.

'After him Alan,' snapped Laxton, reaching out to steady himself against the door frame as he lost his balance.

Billings reached out to detain the man as he came towards him, to no avail; he was thrust aside, finishing up on his backside on the wet driveway as Fulbek made a dash for the car, a blue Austin Maestro that stood on the driveway. There was the sound of the car's engine revving up before it reversed at speed up the drive and out on to the lane; a few seconds later it was disappearing into the distance, but not before he had taken the registration number.

'Get to the car Alan and send a message to all police vehicles in the vicinity, giving a description of the car,' ordered the inspector.

Billings dashed up the drive and on to the lane to where the police car was parked.

A couple of minutes later he returned and informed Laxton that the local police had been alerted. Janet Fulbek was sobbing uncontrollably as the inspector turned his attention to her.

'Now then Mrs Fulbek,' he began sternly. 'I want you to answer a few questions regarding the abduction of young children.'

The little woman, who Laxton judged to be in her mid-forties, was wiping her eyes with her handkerchief; she looked up at him nervously.

'I can't tell you anything,' she croaked, shaking her head from side to side.

'Are you telling me that you are refusing to say anything?' the inspector put to her.

She nodded her head.

'I can't... I daren't,' she said, her voice muffled by the handkerchief.

Laxton, looking down at the shaking woman, stroked his chin, deep in thought for a few seconds before informing her, 'In that case Mrs Fulbek, we will have to take you into custody.'

As Laxton waited for her to gather a few necessities, he noticed a photograph of a couple on the sideboard.

'You and your husband?' he enquired, picking it up and taking a close look at it.

'Yes,' she replied, adding as an afterthought, 'it was taken three years ago.'

He passed it to Billings, telling him, 'We'll take this for identification purposes.'

She looked up at him a concerned expression on her face.

'It will be returned to you as soon as we have taken a copy of your husband's picture,' he assured her as they made their way to the door.

With this she locked the door and dutifully followed the two detectives out of the cottage and up the garden path. Curtains in the other cottages could be seen being pulled back as Janet Fulbek was ushered into the rear seat of the police car. A few seconds later they drove off.

The inspector, who was in the passenger seat, picked up the car phone and enquired whether Martin Fulbek had been detained; the reply was negative. It seemed that he had disappeared.

Eventually they arrived back at headquarters. Mrs Fulbek was taken into the outer office where Bellows and the young policewoman led her to a back room. Laxton and Billings went into the main office where Chief Inspector Wilberton was waiting for them.

'Now then Robert, what have we got?' he put to the inspector, as he and his partner took a seat.

Laxton then gave a detailed description of the happenings at the cottage in Frithville. After listening carefully to what the inspector had to say, Wilberton, his arms folded, sat for a few seconds, his eyes half closed as he absorbed the information.

Suddenly he straightened up.

'We'll have a word with Mrs Fulbek,' he declared, getting to his feet, then, followed by the two officers he went to the back room to where the little woman was being kept.

Janet Fulbek was sipping a cup of tea when they entered.

'Are you being well looked after my dear?' enquired the chief in a somewhat condescending tone of voice.

She nodded her head as she looked up at Wilberton over the rim of her cup. A few seconds later she placed the empty cup on a table in front of her.

'Now then Mrs Fulbek I want you to answer a few questions regarding the children that you had in your keep around sixteen years ago,' he put to her.

Her blue eyes were wide as she looked nervously from one of the policemen to the other that was in front of her. It was obvious that she was scared as she spluttered, 'I... I'm afraid I can't tell you anything.'

'What are you afraid of?' enquired Laxton, leaning forward and looking deep into her eyes.

She turned away without saying anything, shaking her head.

'It will go a lot easier for you if you answer a few questions,' he put to her in a soft voice as he attempted to induce her to speak.

'What do you want to know?' she whispered through her handkerchief.

Laxton looked Wilberton in the eyes. It seemed as though they were getting somewhere at last. He turned his attention back to the woman.

'Is it true that you cashed cheques, each valued at two thousand pounds?'

Janet Fulbek was silent for a moment, before shaking her head and saying, 'No.'

'But we've got the cheques that you cashed,' declared Laxton, a little forcefully.

'I didn't cash them,' she muttered, almost as if to herself.

He leaned a little closer before saying sharply, 'Who did?'

'It was my husband, I never saw any cheques.'

Wilberton pulled up a chair and sat facing her. 'What can you tell me about the children?' he asked her.

She held out her arms in a gesture of futility. 'All I did was look after them,' she declared.

'How long were you supposed to look after the children?' asked Wilberton, leaning forward and clasping his hands in front of him.

'Until someone had signed an agreement to take them,' she replied, adding almost as an afterthought: 'The clients were well vetted before the group would let the children go.'

The police officers exchanged meaningful glances.

'Group,' they both repeated in unison. 'What do you mean by group?'

The woman's hand went to her mouth as she realised that she had said too much.

'It was just a figure of speech,' she explained lamely.

Laxton chewed on his lip as he thought over what she had said before again looking her in the eyes.

'Did you and your husband abduct the children personally?' he grated, his voice full of feeling.

'No,' she told him with a shake of her head, explaining that the children were brought to them by a man and a woman.

'The children were upset at first but they soon settled down after we explained to them that their parents had passed away and that we were going to find them a new mum and dad who would love them.'

'How long did you have them?'

'Oh, I would say the longest was with us for about six months,' she rejoined.

'Were those four children the only ones you had in your care?' asked Billings, getting in on the act.

'Yes,' she replied with a nod of her head.

At that moment Wilberton got to his feet and declared, 'That will do for now.'

'What about me?' enquired Janet Fulbek. 'Can I go home now?'

The chief shook his head.

'I'm afraid not,' he told her a little sharply. 'You will have to be kept in custody until you have told us everything you know regarding these abductions.'

'What am I to do about my meals?' she enquired a little plaintively.

'WPC Johnson will bring you a meal in shortly,' he told her as he and his two officers prepared to leave the room.

'How long are you going to keep me here?' she persisted.

'As I've already told you, until we are satisfied that

you have told us everything regarding the abductions,' he replied, adding as he was about to close the door: 'We'll talk again this afternoon.'

Laxton checked his watch, it was almost one o'clock. He turned to Billings.

'We'll nip for some lunch Alan,' he declared, as they left the chief and set off walking the two hundred yards or so to the nearest chip shop-cum-café which was situated in the centre of Lincoln.

After a quick meal of fish and chips and a mug of coffee, they were sufficiently fortified for the walk back to the station.

Martin Fulbek put his foot down on the accelerator as he sped away from the cottage in Frithville, his mind was in a whirl as he drove to Newark. On arrival in the centre of the town he swiftly parked up and made his way to the nearest telephone box, where he dialled Wooding's number, there was no reply. He tut-tutted impatiently as he dialled another number.

'Hello,' a man's voice intoned.

'Is that Ronald Miller?' enquired Fulbek gruffly.

'Yes,' the voice replied a little sharply. 'Who's asking?'

'Martin Fulbek,' he replied.

There was a long pause before Miller repeated questioningly, 'Martin Fulbek?'

'Yes,' he repeated testily, telling him that Thomas Wooding was supposed to be arranging new accommodation for him and Janet. He then went on to inform him that the police were at their cottage making enquiries about them.

'Mmm,' mumbled Miller. 'It seems something must have happened recently.'

'Not through me and my wife it hasn't,' Fulbek insisted.

'Well something must have gone awry,' was the reply.

'Ever since the children left us everything has gone smoothly,' Fulbek put to him firmly, before going on to inform him of the accident in which the Mallings had lost their lives.

There was a few seconds pause before Miller went on to tell him that he couldn't see how the accident would affect them.

'Then tell me – why are the police making enquiries?' retorted Fulbek.

'That is something that I will have to look into,' was the sharp reply.

'In the meantime what am I supposed to do?' enquired Fulbek.

There was another long pause then Miller asked him, 'Where are you now?'

'I'm in Newark. My car is parked up in the market place in the town centre,' Fulbek muttered before going on to explain that he would have to abandon it as the police would have got the number.

'Stay where you are, I'll be down there shortly to pick you up,' Miller informed him. A few seconds later the phone went dead.

Fulbek put the receiver back on its cradle before stepping out of the phone booth and standing in a prominent position. After twenty minutes had gone by a smart Rover pulled up close to where he was standing. A stockily built man, who looked to be in his late fifties was sat in the driving seat; he nodded his head at Martin Fulbek and told him to climb in.

Chapter 10

'Right, we'll carry on with questioning Mrs Fulbek,' Wilberton asserted as the two officers returned from their meal.

Getting to his feet he walked from behind his desk and made his way to the back room where Janet Fulbek was being kept, followed by Laxton and Billings.

'Now then Mrs Fulbek, I trust you have been well looked after,' he announced, a smile on his face, as they entered the room.

'I can't grumble,' she rejoined with a slight nod of her head as the three officers took their seats opposite her.

The chief, a stern expression on his face, leaned forward and clasped his hands in front of him; directing his attention to the woman, he looked her straight in the eyes as he asked her if one of the girls who she had in her care was named Elizabeth Watling.

Her eyes opened wide with shock on hearing the name.

'How did you…?' she gasped.

'Never mind that for now!' exclaimed the chief, holding his hand up as he went on to ask her: 'What were the names of the other three children that were with you?'

She leaned forward, her face in her hands as she sobbed uncontrollably.

Laxton reached into his top pocket, took out a handkerchief and handed it to her.

She nodded her thanks as she dabbed her eyes.

Wilberton leaned back and waited patiently for her to settle down before repeating his question, albeit in a softer tone of voice. 'Now then Mrs Fulbek, in your own time tell us the children's true names.'

Janet Fulbek carefully dabbed her eyes as she took in what the chief inspector had said to her.

'I'm sorry I can't remember off hand,' she mumbled, shaking her head slowly from side to side.

'It's obvious that you recalled the name of Elizabeth Watling,' he told her before going on to ask her a little forcefully: 'Do the names Gateland, Benning and Batley mean anything to you?'

She paused for few seconds as she looked up at him over her hand-held handkerchief.

'It was such a long time ago,' she confided with a slight shake of her head. 'It's difficult to recall the children's names.'

'Surely you remember the children Mrs Fulbek,' Laxton put to her, adding a little sarcastically, 'One of your neighbours, a Mrs Goldsworthy, recalled the children and the time when you had them, quite well.'

'I... I can't tell you, I daren't,' she sobbed, again burying her face in the handkerchief.

'As I've told you before Mrs Fulbek, you will be kept in custody until we are convinced that you have told us all you know,' declared the chief as he got to his feet and announced: 'We'll leave it there for the moment.'

He was deep in thought as he left the room and returned to his office, followed closely by the two detectives. After instructing Bellows to send in three coffees he turned to Laxton.

'Robert I want you to return to the Fulbek's address in Frithville and check if there is anything there that will indicate where the other three children may be.' He paused for a moment before going on to tell him, 'I'll inform Boston headquarters that you will be there today.'

He opened the drawer in his desk and took out a bunch of keys that had been taken from Janet Fulbek. Handing them to Laxton he told him, 'These are the keys to the Fulbeks' cottage.'

Laxton acknowledged him with a nod of his head as he reached out and took the keys from him before placing them in his pocket.

At that moment WPC Johnson came through the door carrying three coffees on a tray, which she placed on the desk. They each nodded their thanks before picking them up.

'We'll get down there right away,' Laxton informed the chief before blowing on his coffee a couple of times and taking a sip.

Ten minutes later he and Billings left the building

and made their way to the car. Laxton tossed the keys to his partner with a, 'You drive.'

He was deep in thought as they joined the busy main highway on their way to Frithville. An hour later they had passed through Sibsey; a sign came up indicating Frithville to the right. Another ten minutes and they were drawing up outside the Fulbeks' home. One or two curtains moved in the nearby cottages as they climbed out of the car and walked down the path to the side door. After trying a couple of keys the door opened and the two detectives entered the cottage.

'I think we'll start on the upper floor Alan,' said Laxton as he proceeded to climb the stairs that were in the hallway. Reaching the top he saw that there were two bedrooms; turning to Billings he instructed him to search the back bedroom and he would search the front one. Twenty minutes later he stood with his hands on his hips, a look of frustration on his face.

'Nothing in there,' he declared.

Billings was just coming out of the other bedroom.

'Nothing in there either,' he rejoined with a shake of his head.

'Never mind, we've still got the downstairs rooms to look through,' declared Laxton a little hopefully as he placed his hand on the bannister and made his way carefully down the steep stairs followed by his partner.

Laxton rummaged through the drawers and cupboards in the old fashioned sideboard, scrutinising every piece of paper carefully; Billings was doing likewise in the kitchen. After half an hour had gone by it was obvious to the inspector, that if there was any evidence it was going to be hard to uncover. He joined his partner in the kitchen who told him that he also hadn't had any luck.

Laxton opened the curtain and glanced through the window.

'What's this?' he said, his brow furrowed questioningly, as he saw that there was a conservatory attached to the rear of the cottage, a back door led to it.

'Might as well check it over,' he decided without much conviction as they went through the door and entered the somewhat dilapidated structure that ran along the rear of the garage making it much larger than the kitchen.

Laxton stood for a few seconds as he cast his eyes over the two wickerwork chairs and table that were the only pieces of furniture. There was a heavy wooden door in the rear wall of the property, near the far end of the conservatory.

'I wonder what's in here?' he muttered as he strode over to the door, reached out for the handle and gave it a push. The door was locked.

'Looks as though it leads into the back of the garage,' suggested Billings.

'You are probably right,' rejoined the inspector; he had a thoughtful expression on his lean face as he turned to his young partner. 'Do any of those keys fit it Alan?' he enquired.

Billings reached into his pocket and took out the keys. After selecting them one at a time, he came to the final one. He gave a sigh of relief, it fitted. Swinging the door open they stepped inside, expecting to find themselves in the rear of the garage. They couldn't have been more wrong. A room had been created by bricking off a third of the garage. There was a switch on the wall. Laxton reached up and clicked it on. There was a pause before a fluorescent light flickered on. He cast his eyes round what looked to be a well-equipped office; he nodded his head in approval as he took in the typewriter, printer and telephone. A small metal safe stood on the sturdy desk. It was locked. After carefully checking through the drawers and finding nothing, he turned to Billings and again asked him, 'Do any of the keys fit this safe Alan?'

The young man checked through the bunch of keys. He shook his head. 'No,' he replied.

Laxton studied the situation for a moment.

'I reckon we will have to get some advice on our next move,' he muttered.

Reaching out for the phone which stood on the desk, he rang headquarters. Bellows answered it.

'Put me on to the chief,' he requested.

A couple of seconds later a voice said, 'Hello.'

Laxton went on to explain to him that they had discovered the safe and wanted to know if they would be in order taking it away from the property as it was locked and there was no key for it.

'Mmm,' muttered the chief as he thought over the problem for a few seconds, before adding: 'Leave it with me for fifteen minutes. I'll get back to you.'

There was click as he put the phone down, Laxton followed suit.

'What have we got to do?' enquired Billings as the inspector turned away from the phone.

'The chief's looking into it. He's ringing us back.'

After what seemed an interminable time the phone rang.

Laxton picked it up; it was the chief. He told him that under the circumstances, he would be in order taking the safe out of the property and bringing it with him. Laxton nodded his head at the receiver, thanked him and put the phone down before turning to Billings and informing him, 'It looks as though we will be able to take it with us.'

Billings reached out and hefted the safe on to his shoulder before striding through the cottage and out onto the driveway. Laxton took the keys from him, locked up and followed him to the car. After he had opened the boot the breathless young man carefully lowered the heavy safe into it; banging the boot lid down they climbed into the car. A few minutes later they were making their way through the village, to the obligatory flutter of the neighbours' curtains.

It was just beginning to spot with rain as they neared Lincoln; the 'Three Sisters', poked up out of the mist as they approached the city centre. The chief was waiting for them when they arrived at police headquarters; a couple of constables were on hand to take the safe into the rear office where a locksmith was waiting. A few minutes later the safe was open. Laxton reached inside it and took out numerous rolled up documents secured by elastic bands and placed them on the table in front of a seated Wilberton.

'Now let's see what we've got here,' muttered the chief as he reached out and picked up one of the documents. After carefully running his eyes over it, he looked over the rim of his glasses at Laxton, his brow deeply furrowed as he handed the document over to him, saying sombrely, 'Read this and give me your opinion.'

The inspector reached out, picked up the document and read it, an ever deepening frown forming on his forehead as he absorbed its contents. The document told of a carefully thought out plan to abduct young children and sell them to childless couples for a sum of ten thousand pounds. It stipulated that we're not be harmed in any way and that they were to be treated with care.

'It does say one thing. The children who were abducted are probably still alive somewhere,' intoned Laxton, placing the document back on the table in front of the chief before leaning back in his chair, his arms folded.

'I think it would be a good idea for us to have another word with Janet Fulbek,' declared Wilberton.

Fifteen minutes later the woman was brought into the room and given a seat, where she sat nervously as the chief ran his eyes over the papers that were strewn on the table in front of him.

After a few seconds had gone by, he took off his glasses and held them in his hand as he looked at her; he had a serious expression on his face as he informed her in a low voice, 'These documents were found at your home in Frithville; they seem to indicate that you had children staying with you.'

He paused for a moment before going on to tell her, 'I want you to explain in your own words what you know about the children that were abducted in nineteen sixty-eight.'

The little woman sat back in her seat, her eyes half

closed and her hands clasped in her lap as she thought over carefully what the chief inspector had said.

'As I've already told you, I can't tell you anything more than I already have,' she insisted with a shake of her head.

Wilberton reached out, picked up the document in question and held it out, stating, 'Is it true that you had four children in your care in nineteen sixty-eight – sixty-nine?'

Janet Fulbek took a deep breath before suddenly coming to a decision.

'Yes it's true, we did have four children in our care during the period that you stated,' she admitted before adding with a shake of her head, 'but I had not been told that they had been abducted.'

Laxton addressed the woman. 'Can you tell us where the children went to after they left you?'

The woman was taken a little aback at the question, pausing for a moment before going on to say adamantly, 'I can't tell you.'

'Does that mean that you know where they have gone and that you won't say?' the inspector put to her a little sharply.

She didn't answer, her head dropping as she buried her face in her hands. It was obvious that his question had hit home. There was a pause in the interrogation as the woman's shoulders heaved.

'Would you like a hot drink?' enquired the chief in a softer tone of voice. She nodded her head, muttering, 'Tea please.'

Wilberton looked across at Billings and instructed him to inform Sergeant Bellows to send in three coffees and a cup of tea. The young man got to his feet and disappeared into the outer office. He returned a couple of minutes later and nodded his head at the chief as he took his seat.

'Now then Mrs Fulbek, does the name Malling mean anything to you?' enquired Wilberton, assuming a more friendly attitude.

The woman's back visibly stiffened as she heard the name; she paused for a few seconds before replying in a soft voice, 'I do recall a couple of that name taking one of the children.'

'Do you remember the name of the child before she was, er, adopted?' Laxton put to her, a serious expression on his face as he sat forward in his seat.

'I think she told us her name was Elizabeth, er, Wadling or was it Watling?' she muttered, her brow furrowed as she juggled the two names.

At that moment the young WPC came in the room carrying a tray with the drinks on it. The officers nodded their thanks as she placed the tray on the table and withdrew.

'What about the other three children that was in your care; do you recall their names?' asked the chief, eyeing her over the rim of his glasses as he reached out and picked up one of the mugs of coffee.

Janet Fulbek sipped at her tea, a thoughtful expression on her face as she cast her mind back over the years.

'As far as I can recollect there were another two girls and a boy,' she mumbled as she dabbed her mouth with her handkerchief.

Wilberton put it to her again, 'Do you recall their names?'

She half closed her eyes for a few seconds as she cast her mind back before telling him in a quiet tone of voice, 'The other two girls names were Caroline Gateland and Margaret Benning. The little boy's name was Jonathan Batley,' she said firmly.

'How did you come by their names?' he persisted.

'The children told me themselves over the time that they were with us,' she replied.

'What did you do to make them forget their parents?' asked Laxton, breaking in on the chief's line of questioning.

She shrugged her shoulders before telling them that they had convinced the children that their parents had passed away and that they were going to be looked after by new ones.

'Do you know the names of the couples who adopted them?' he put to her.

'I'm afraid I wasn't privy to that information,' she rejoined, shaking her head.

'Can you tell us where the group that were running the, er, scam, were situated.'

She gave an almost imperceptible shrug of her small shoulders.

'All I can tell you is that any contact my husband had with them always seemed to be from the Nottingham area,' she told them in a quiet voice.

'Right!' exclaimed Wilberton, slapping the table top with the palm of his hands. 'That will do for the moment.'

Pushing his chair back and getting to his feet he called for the WPC to take Janet Fulbek back to her room.

'How long are you intending to keep me here?' the woman enquired a little sharply as she was about to be led away.

The chief stroked his chin for a few seconds as he mulled over her question before informing her, 'When we are sure that you have given us all the information regarding the abduction of the children, then you will be allowed to return home.'

On this note she was led away. The chief, Laxton and Billings made their way out of the room and back to the main office.

'What we've got to find out is some connection to the abductors,' announced an exasperated Wilberton as he took his seat at the back of the desk; reaching out, he picked up his glasses and put them on before again running his eyes carefully over the documents that were in the safe that the two officers had brought with them from the cottage in Frithville.

At that moment the phone rang; the chief picked up the receiver – it was Sergeant Bellows in the outer office informing him of a call from the Newark police.

'Okay Sergeant, put it through,' he directed.

The call was a message to inform them that a blue Austin Maestro with the aforesaid number plate had been discovered by the local car park attendant; it was parked on the main car park in Newark, adding that it didn't have a current parking ticket on it.

Wilberton thanked the officer, telling him to give instructions that the car was not to be moved and that they would send someone to check it over.

'What was that all about?' enquired an inquisitive Laxton.

Wilberton explained to him that Fulbek's car had been found and that he wanted the inspector to look into it. A few minutes later Laxton, accompanied by Billings, was on his way to Newark. On arrival they were met by one of the local transport police who had been keeping his eye on the vehicle. The inspector nodded his head at the big well-built officer as he and Billings approached the car in question. Laxton tried the door, it was locked. The uniformed policeman stepped forward with a metal lever and forced open the window; he gave a satisfied grunt as he reached inside and unlocked the door before swinging it open.

'There you are sir,' he declared, an expression of satisfaction at his achievement on his face as he stood back from the car.

Laxton smiled as he nodded his head at the officer and thanked him before stepping forward and leaning into the car. Reaching over the back of the seat he opened the rear door, telling his partner, 'Check out the rear of the car Alan.'

Billings climbed into the car and proceeded to do as ordered; in the meantime the inspector was giving the front of the car a thorough going over. Ten minutes later he sat back a look of frustration on his face as he turned to his partner.

'Have you found anything Alan?' he enquired from his position in the driver's seat.

Billings shook his head.

'Nothing back here,' he announced with a shrug of his shoulders.

'Mmm,' mumbled Laxton, shaking his head disappointedly. 'It looks as though we've drawn a blank.'

He was just about to get out of the car when he reached up and pulled down the sun shield. A card was slotted into a small pocket that was on the back of it.

'What's this?' he muttered to himself as he took it out and looked at it. There was a number written on the card. It had obviously been placed there as a reminder.

Billings stuck his head over the back seat. 'It might be a phone number,' he offered.

'Quite possibly Alan, quite possibly,' he rejoined, before informing him: 'We'll check it out when we get back to headquarters.'

After thanking the officer who was keeping his eye on the vehicle, they climbed into their car and set off back to Lincoln. On arrival they went straight into the chief's office.

'Any luck?' enquired Wilberton, looking up at them over the rim of his glasses, as they approached his desk.

'Not much,' declared Laxton with a slight shake of his head, as he and his partner each pulled up a chair and sat down.

'So you did find something then?' the chief put to them, a note of expectancy in his voice.

'Only this,' replied the inspector, tossing the card with the number on it, onto the desk.

Wilberton reached out, picked it up and studied it for a couple of seconds before enquiring, 'What do you think it is?'

Laxton shrugged his shoulders.

'Could be a telephone number,' he replied, before

going on to say: 'The problem is there isn't any code in front of the number.'

The chief plucked at the lobe of his ear as he studied the situation.

'Janet Fulbek did say that the connections seemed to be from the Nottingham area,' he suggested.

'There is one way to find out Chief,' piped up Billings.

Wilberton looked up at the young man, a half smile on his face as he conceded, 'You may be right Constable.'

Reaching out for the phone he dialled the Nottingham code before adding the six digit number written on the card. He leaned back in his seat as he waited for a reply. After what seemed an eternity someone picked up the phone. A man's gruff voice said, 'Hello.'

'Who am I speaking to?' enquired the chief, sharply.

The phone suddenly went dead.

Wilberton looked at the receiver for a few seconds before saying grimly, 'Gentlemen I reckon we are on to something.'

He directed his gaze at Billings.

'Tell Bellows I want him will you Constable?'

Billings jumped to his feet and went out of the door. A few seconds later he was back in followed by Sergeant Bellows.

'Yes Chief what is it you want?' enquired the big man.

Wilberton wrote the Nottingham code in front of the number that was written on the card, before handing it to Bellows, instructing him, 'Get in touch with the telephone authorities and ask them to trace this number Sergeant.'

Bellows took it from him before leaving the room and going into his office.

The chief rubbed the palms of his hands together vigorously in anticipation of what the inquiry may produce, before addressing the two officers.

'We may be getting somewhere at last,' he declared, a grim smile on his face.

Laxton, his hands clasped in front of him had a thoughtful expression on his face as he addressed the chief. 'I think it might be a good time to have another word with, Mrs Fulbek.'

'I tend to agree with you, Robert,' rejoined Wilberton before getting to his feet and making his way to the interrogation room once again; Laxton and his partner dutifully followed him. After informing Bellows of their intentions they took a seat and waited; after a few minutes had gone by WPC Johnson came into the room with Janet Fulbek, who took a seat in front them.

'When am I going to be allowed to go home?' she enquired plaintively, a troubled expression on her face.

Wilberton held his hand up before telling her, 'All in good time Mrs Fulbek. First of all I have to tell you that we have received certain information with regard to your husband.'

The woman, her brow deeply creased, looked him straight in the eyes as she asked him in a low voice, 'And what would that be?'

'We've located his car in a car park in Newark and

we have reason to believe that he may be in the Nottingham area.' He paused for a moment before asking her pointedly, 'Do you know of any address that he may be staying at?'

Her face visibly blanched at the mention of Nottingham.

'I... I don't recall Martin ever mentioning Nottingham,' she muttered a little unconvincingly, with a slight shake of her head.

At that moment Bellows came in and handed him a sheet of paper. On it was written, 16 Blexley Road, Beeston, Nottingham. Wilberton studied it for a couple of seconds, before turning to her and enquiring, 'Have you heard of an address at Beeston, in Nottingham?'

There was no reply from her; she had a grim expression on her face as she looked down at her small hands which were clasping and unclasping nervously in her lap. The chief leaned forward, his elbows on the table, his fingers forming a pyramid.

'You might as well tell us all you know Mrs Fulbek,' he advised her, lowering his voice as he did so.

After a long pause she looked up at him, a beaten expression on her face.

'There isn't a lot I can add to the information that I've already told you,' she confided, her voice almost a whisper.

There was another long pause before she told them that her husband was the one who did all the organising.

'Were the four children brought to you together?' enquired Laxton.

She turned to him, a questioning frown on her forehead. He could see that she didn't quite understand what he was getting at. He tried another tack.

'What I mean is, were they brought to you one at a time or as a group?' he explained.

'Oh I see what you mean,' she rejoined, giving a slight nod of her head before going on to explain. 'They were delivered to us one at a time.'

'At regular intervals?' the inspector put to her.

'Not really,' she replied, adding with a shrug of her shoulders: 'There was a week, sometimes two weeks between them.'

'What are you getting at Robert?' queried the chief, a perplexed look on his face.

'I'm trying to ascertain if they were delivered to them as they were abducted or were they being held at another address before being placed with the Fulbeks as a group,' Laxton explained, before putting to the chief that it was possible that the abductors may have taken other children.

'Mmm,' muttered Wilberton. 'You may have something there.'

He turned his attention back to Janet Fulbek.

'Did the people who brought the children to you ever mention anything regarding having abducted other children?'

She shook her head.

'No,' she replied emphatically.

The chief crossed his arms and chewed on his bottom lip for a few seconds before turning once again to the woman in front of him.

'Have you any idea whatsoever where the children were being held before they came to you?'

She shook her head slowly from side to side before replying in a quiet voice, 'All I can tell you is that Martin was contacted by someone who asked him if he could accommodate four children for a short while.'

She looked into the chief's eyes and explained to him with a shrug of her shoulders that was all she knew about them until later, when her husband explained to her that the children were to be found caring adoptive parents.

'Did he mention any names?' queried Laxton, leaning towards her.

'I'm afraid not,' she replied firmly.

'What about the Nottingham connection. What do you know about that?' He paused for a moment before adding, 'It seems that your husband made a call from the phone box near where his car was found. The call was to a person in Beeston.'

Her eyes widened as she heard the name of the town in the Nottingham area.

'So you do know what I'm talking about,' he told her a little sharply.

She dropped her head into her hands; her shoulders slumped as she muttered, 'It's no use me denying everything Inspector, my husband has mentioned an address in Beeston.'

Laxton looked across at Wilberton. The chief nodded his head and they both walked out of the room and into the main office. He turned to Laxton, informing him, 'It looks as though we are getting somewhere at last.'

He paused for a moment and looked at his watch;

it showed four forty-five.

'I think it would be a good idea to get to that Beeston address as soon as you can tomorrow morning Robert and see what you can come up with. In the meantime I'll contact police headquarters in Nottingham and let them know that you will be coming.'

He paused for a moment, his eyes half closed.

'Now let me see, the last time that I was in touch with Nottingham, Chief Inspector David Jenkins was in charge.'

'Taffy Jenkins?' queried Laxton. 'I haven't seen him since we were together in training.'

He shook his head as he recalled the big ginger haired freckle-faced fellow recruit. Wilberton picked up the phone and dialled the Nottingham number.

Laxton went back into the interviewing room and nodded at Billings who had been sat with the woman. Billings got to his feet and followed the inspector out of the room as Janet Fulbek was escorted back to the cells.

'What now boss?' he grunted as he closed the door behind him.

Laxton suppressed a smile at the term that the young constable had used as they exited the police station.

'We'll check the address in Beeston first thing tomorrow morning,' he informed his partner as they made their way to his car.

Half an hour later he dropped Billings off at his home before carrying on to Old Bolingbroke. Annie was just coming out of the door as he pulled up in the driveway.

'Your dinner is in the oven Mr Laxton,' she called out at the top of her voice as he climbed out of the car.

He smiled his thanks and waved his hand as he went to the door. After a shower and a good rub down he felt a new man as he went downstairs fastening his dressing gown.

'Now let me see what culinary delight Annie has cooked for me!' he exclaimed as he opened the oven door and took out the two large plates that enclosed his dinner. Placing them on the table he took the top plate off, uncovering two large pork chops, new potatoes and cabbage.

'Bless you Annie,' he muttered as he picked up the knife and fork and tucked in.

Chapter 11

There wasn't a cloud in the sky and the morning sun was just beginning to show over the surrounding hills of Old Bolingbroke as Inspector Laxton negotiated the steep, winding narrow lane that led from the sleepy village to the main road. He gave a deep sigh of contentment as he cast his eyes over the open countryside; he could make out the cattle peacefully grazing between the gaps in bushes that lined the fields as he sped along on his journey to Wragby, where he was to pick up his young partner.

Alan Billings was standing on the pathway outside his home waiting for Laxton as the car drew up beside him. He gave a wave of his hand and a, 'Good morning,' as he approached the vehicle.

The inspector got out of the car, tossed him the keys and instructed him to drive before he climbed into the passenger seat.

'We'll call in at the Nottingham police headquarters,' he told his partner as he fastened his seatbelt.

Two minutes later they were on their way to Nottingham. The inspector laid his head back as he thought over the recent events as Billings carefully drove through the busy traffic on his way along the outskirts of Lincoln; after around thirty minutes travelling along the A46 the sign depicting Newark-on-Trent came into view. He smiled to himself as he cast his mind back to the many pleasant hours he had spent fishing from the banks of the wide river. He looked down at its calm surface as they drove over the bridge. Lifting his arm, he checked his watch; it was nine thirty.

'I reckon we should be there somewhere around quarter past ten Alan,' he told his young partner, before settling back in his seat, his arms folded, enjoying the open countryside as it flashed by.

Forty minutes later they entered the busy Nottingham city centre; another ten minutes and they were turning into the large headquarters car park. Climbing out of the car they entered the main entrance. They were met by a young looking policewoman, her blonde hair trimmed short. 'Can I help you gentlemen?' she enquired, a smile on her pretty face.

Laxton explained to her who they were and that they wished to speak to Chief Inspector Jenkins.

'Come this way Inspector,' she trilled as she led them to a door at the back of reception. Giving a sharp knock, she opened the door and stuck her head round it.

'Inspector Laxton to see you sir,' she announced, pushing the door open as she did so, before standing back and letting the two officers through.

'Ahh Robert, it's good to see you again,' gushed the heavily built ginger-haired chief inspector; he had a broad smile on his, creased, still freckled face as he got to his feet and made his way round the desk, his hand outstretched.

Laxton matched the big man's smile before grabbing the hand and shaking it vigorously.

'It's been a long time Dave,' he said a little huskily, his feelings overwhelming him a little as he and his partner took a seat in front of the desk, Jenkins returning to his seat.

'Must be all of twenty-eight years!' the chief exclaimed, shaking his head in wonderment as he leaned forward, his elbows resting on the desk, his hands clasped in front of him.

'Now then Robert, Chief Inspector Wilberton informed me that you were coming. What's it all about?' he enquired, his brow furrowed.

Laxton explained to him that they were investigating the abduction of the four children in 1968 or thereabouts.

'Mmm, I recollect something about that incident,' Jenkins muttered, leaning back and running his fingers through his thinning hair. 'If I remember correctly, they never did find them.'

Laxton nodded his head before going on to tell him of the facts so far, indicating that they may have come up with evidence that pointed to the people staying at the property situated at number 16 Blexley Road, Beeston being involved.

Jenkins stroked his chin for a few seconds before suddenly coming to a decision.

'Right Robert, I'll go along with you.'

Jumping to his feet, he went to the door, opened it and called out, 'WPC Jennings.'

A few seconds later the young blonde haired policewoman came through the door.

'Yes sir,' she replied sharply.

'Get the car ready will you, I'll be out in a couple of minutes?' he asked her before turning and addressing Laxton and Billings. 'Robert I think it would be better for you to follow us,' he informed them, adding as he made for the door, 'we know the way.'

Laxton nodded his head in agreement as he and his partner followed the big man out to the car park where the policewoman was sat patiently waiting in a police car; the chief, after checking again with Laxton, the address in Beeston, climbed into the passenger seat of the police car. Laxton and Billings followed suit by getting into their car. A couple of minutes later they were following the police vehicle out of the car park. After a tedious time-consuming journey through the busy thoroughfare of Nottingham, they eventually arrived at Beeston. The house they were looking for was a terraced property among a row of ex-pit houses. They stopped outside number sixteen. Curtains in adjoining properties could be seen being pulled back as the two vehicles, one of them the police car, pulled up. After instructing WPC Jennings to wait in the car the chief disembarked and led the other two officers down the short path that was in front of number sixteen. Billings hammered on the door with his clenched fist; after waiting for a few seconds he banged on the door again.

'All right! All right! Don't knock the bloody door

down,' a gruff voice called out as the key turned in the lock.

The door opened slowly, a short man just over five feet tall who looked to be in his late fifties, stood in the doorway. He looked up at the tall officers, a belligerent expression on his unshaven face as they identified themselves.

'What can I do for you?' he enquired sharply; he obviously wasn't overawed by what he was confronted with.

'And your name is sir?' enquired Billings, note book in hand.

'Finchley,' the small man replied adding, a little grudgingly, 'Alfred Finchley.'

He stuck his head out of the door and quickly glanced up and down the street.

'You'd better come in,' he told them, stepping back as he did so.

After closing the door behind them he led them along a short passageway into a back room.

Laxton wrinkled his nose at the smell of stale tobacco as they made themselves comfortable on an old settee and a couple of chairs, Chief Inspector Jenkins nodded his head indicating to Laxton that he should start the questioning.

'Now then Mr Finchley, first of all are you acquainted with a couple named Fulbek?' enquired the inspector.

The little man scratched his scraggy greying hair, a puzzled expression on his face.

'Fulbek, Fulbek,' he muttered, half to himself. 'Never heard the name,' he said with a shake of his head.

Laxton reached into his pocket and took out a photograph. It was a copy of Martin Fulbek taken from the photograph that they had come across at the home of Janet Fulbek. He held it out to Finchley.

'Do you recognise that man?' he enquired pointedly.

The little man took the photograph from him and studied it for a few seconds, his brown eyes half closed as he stroked his fingers along his rather long nose.

'I do recall him staying here for one night,' he confided in a low voice, adding: 'One of my regulars brought him and asked if he could stay overnight.'

He gave a shrug of his shoulders.

'He was gone the next morning,' he grunted.

'Have you any idea where he went to?'

I'm afraid I don't,' replied the little man.

'The person who asked you to take him in, is he in at the moment?' enquired the inspector.

Finchley gave a shrug of his shoulders.

'He went out about an hour ago,' he replied, adding: 'He didn't say when he would be back.'

'What is his name?'

'Ronald, er Ronald Miller,' Finchley replied a little hesitantly.

Chief Inspector Jenkins butted in. 'I think it would be a good idea for us to have a look round his room. Have you a spare key?'

Finchley was taken aback at the suggestion, telling the officer, 'Yes I've got a spare key but I don't think it would be right to enter his room without his permission.'

'We'll worry about that Mr Finchley,' was the sharp reply as the little man reluctantly took a key from a hook on the wall and handed it to the chief, telling him: 'It's the first door at the top of the stairs.'

The three officers trooped up the stairs and stopped outside the aforementioned door. Jenkins led them into the gloomy, rather dingy room. A single unmade bed stood in the corner, beside it was a sideboard and wardrobe combined. A small set of drawers completed the furnishings. Laxton bent down and opened the door of the sideboard and took out a number of envelopes that were laying on one of the shelves; opening them, he ran his eyes carefully over the contents, flicking over the pages as he did so.

'Anything of interest?' asked Jenkins, who was in the process of checking through the pockets of the clothing that was hanging on coat hangers in the wardrobe.

'Nothing that has any connection to what we are looking for,' the inspector replied with a slight shake of his head as he placed the four envelopes that he was holding, back in the drawer.

'What have we got here?' announced Billings, who had been carefully rummaging through the set of drawers.

He was looking through the pages of a note book which he was holding in his hand. Laxton went over to him, a questioning expression on his face.

'Anything interesting?' he enquired.

'It looks like a list of phone numbers and names,' Billings declared, as he passed it to the inspector.

Laxton took the book from him and ran his eyes over it, taking in the half dozen names that were beside the list of phone numbers. His eyes narrowed as he stopped at one of the names on the list. It was Martin Fulbek.

'Mmm, I reckon we are getting somewhere at last,' he declared.

'Have you come up with something?' enquired Jenkins, walking over to him and glancing over his shoulder at the book.

Laxton nodded his head before explaining to him, 'One of the names on the list is Fulbek, that's the surname of the woman who we have in custody at Lincoln.'

'That means that the person who is staying here has some connection with the people who were involved in the abduction of the children,' Jenkins put to him.

'It certainly looks that way,' rejoined the inspector as he carried on studying the list of names.

Suddenly he gave a quick intake of breath.

'Malling!' he exclaimed. 'Isn't that the name of the young woman whose parents were killed in a car accident and found that she had been adopted and was recently reinstated with her true family?'

'Yes that's right, she found out that her true name is Watling,' piped up Billings.

'That means that it is quite possible that some of these other names could be connected to the other three children that we are looking for,' declared Laxton.

After another fifteen minutes or so had gone by they came to the conclusion that there wasn't anything more that they could come up with. Before they left Chief Inspector Jenkins assured Laxton that they would keep the property under surveillance. The owner of the property, Alfred Finchley was instructed to inform the police when the occupier of the room returned. He told them that he would do so.

'I'll take this notebook with me, if it's okay with you Dave?' said Laxton, turning to the chief inspector.

'That'll be okay,' rejoined Jenkins with a nod of his head as they made their way to their respective vehicles. Twenty minutes later they went their different ways. Laxton, who was in the passenger seat, gave a wave of his hand as his old friend turned off for the centre of Nottingham and they joined the A46, the road that would take them to Lincoln. He gave a sigh as he settled down in his seat, his arms folded; around half an hour later they were approaching Newark-on-Trent, the inspector checked his watch, it was one thirty; he was feeling hungry.

'Stop at the first pub you come across Alan, we'll have a bite to eat.'

Billings nodded his head in reply. Five minutes after passing over the bridge he pulled into the car park of the White Lion. Climbing out of the car they entered the glass entrance door.

After taking a seat at one of the tables Laxton ordered two haddock and chips and two teas. Half an hour later, their hunger assuaged, they continued on their journey to Lincoln. Laxton grimaced as he glanced up at the sky. Black clouds were beginning to loom over the cathedral as they approached Lincoln.

'Looks like we are going to get some rain Alan,' grunted the inspector as they negotiated the heavy traffic in the centre of the city. A few minutes later they were turning into the police headquarters car park. Laxton checked his watch before getting out of the car, it was three o'clock. Spots of rain were beginning to show on the windscreen as he sat up in his seat and stretched himself, then accompanied by his partner, the two officers walked across the car park and entered the outer office.

'Good afternoon Inspector,' a smiling Sergeant Bellows greeted them.

'Is the chief busy?' enquired Laxton.

'He's told me to send you straight in when you arrive,' was the reply.

The two officers made their way across the reception and entered the chief's office. Wilberton nodded his head at them and indicated for them to take a seat as they entered the room.

'Now then Robert, what have you come up with?' he enquired.

Laxton took out the note book and passed it to the chief informing him that it had been found in the room of a 'Ronald Miller'.

Wilberton put his glasses on before opening the book and running his eyes carefully over the list of names in it.

'Malling,' he muttered, a questioning expression on his face as he looked over the rim of his glasses at the inspector. 'Wasn't that the name of the adopted girl's father; the one that was killed in the car accident?' he put to him.

Laxton, who was sat with his arms folded, nodded his head in agreement before suggesting to the chief that the one or two of the names on the list may refer to the other children that had been abducted.

'I tend to agree with you,' replied Wilberton, adding: 'I think it would be a good idea to have another word with Janet Fulbek.'

He pressed a button on the intercom that was on his desk and spoke into it. 'Sergeant, can you take Mrs Fulbek to the interviewing room?'

With this the three officers, led by Wilberton, made their way to the aforesaid room.

A couple of minutes later Sergeant Bellows led the annoyed looking woman into the room.

'How much longer am I going to be kept here?' she snapped as she was shown to a seat.

The chief raised his hand in an attempt to console her. 'I can promise you that we will return you back home as soon as you have answered a few more questions,' he assured her.

She took a deep breath before telling him, 'All right, now what is it you want to know?'

The chief, taking a seat opposite her, took out the note book and opened it on the page containing the list of names.

'Do any of these names mean anything to you?' he put to her before commencing to read them out.

Her shoulders sagged; she dropped her face into her hands as some of the names struck home.

'Are some of the names familiar to you?' Wilberton again put to her, lowering his voice as he did so.

She nodded her head.

'Which ones are they?' he asked her, a little more forcefully.

She paused for a moment to compose herself,

before looking into his eyes and telling him, a little chokingly, 'The names Norwood, Rothman and Allinson.'

'What significance do these names have?' enquired Laxton, who had been sitting by quietly absorbing the exchanges.

She turned to him, dabbing her eyes with a handkerchief as she did so.

'They are the names of the ones who adopted them,' she told them.

Laxton and Wilberton looked at each other, the serious expression on their faces showing the significance of the statement from the woman.

'Do you know any of the addresses of these people?' enquired Wilberton, leaning towards her, his hands clasped in front of him.

She shook her head, telling him, 'I'm sorry I don't.'

The chief paused for a few seconds before informing Janet Fulbek that they were through questioning her for the moment and that he was going to allow her to go back home. Getting to his feet he called out for Bellows.

'Yes Chief,' was the sharp response from the big sergeant as he poked his head round the door.

'Sergeant, I want you to get some transport to take Mrs Fulbek back home,' ordered Wilberton.

'Right away Chief,' replied Bellows.

'I'm sorry for any inconvenience you may have suffered Mrs Fulbek!' Wilberton exclaimed as she was escorted out of the room.

A stony-faced Janet Fulbek walked straight past him. There was no reply from her.

'What now Chief?' enquired Laxton as the three of them trooped out of the room and into Wilberton's office.

'First of all we'll check out the phone numbers of the three families who have adopted the three children in question,' he replied as he took his seat behind his desk, reached out for the phone and dialled a number.

'Hello, this is Chief Inspector Wilberton here, can you get me in touch with the department that would be able to trace the address of a phone number,' he enquired.

A few seconds went by before a voice on the other end of the line told him that it would be possible though highly irregular.

'It is in connection with an ongoing investigation,' Wilberton explained.

'What is the phone number of the address you want us to trace?' asked the operator on the other end of the line.

'Well actually there are three addresses we require tracing,' the chief put to him.

'Read the numbers out and I'll check with "the powers that be", and see what can be done.'

Wilberton read out the phone numbers.

'Leave it with us, I'll contact you as soon as we have some results,' the operator told him.

Wilberton placed the phone back on the rest, a thoughtful expression on his face.

'Can they do it?' enquired Laxton.

'They are going to ring me back as soon as they come up with something,' the chief told him.

'Anyway,' he added, looking at his watch, it showed five fifteen. 'There isn't much we can do tonight; we'll have to go into it tomorrow morning.'

With this Laxton and his partner got to their feet, left the office and made their way to the car.

The rain was beginning to come down a little heavier as the inspector carefully manoeuvred the car out of the car park; after negotiating the busy city traffic they were leaving Lincoln behind them. Laxton took his eyes off the road for a few seconds and turned to his young partner. 'Well Alan it seems we are finally getting somewhere,' he put to him.

Billings nodded his head; there was a thoughtful expression on his face as he muttered, 'If the chief gets a good response from the telephone headquarters regarding the phone numbers, we should be able to trace the addresses.'

The inspector gave a grunt of approval at the young man's rational reply.

The rain was beginning to come down heavily and the windscreen wipers were working overtime as they approached Wragby.

'Looks like you will have to make a run for it,' intimated Laxton as he stopped the car outside the young man's front gate.

Billings gave a grimace as he turned his coat collar up; he shouted a quick 'goodbye' before opening the car door and making a dash to the front door which his mother was holding open for him. Laxton gave a wave of his hand before continuing his journey home.

The rain had abated somewhat as he drew into his driveway, climbed out of the car and entered his house. Annie had left a note on the table informing him that his dinner was in the oven. After a quick wash he took out the heaped plate of meat and potato pie from the oven and tucked in with gusto. Fifteen minutes later, a satisfied expression on his face, he leaned back in his chair and patted his stomach. Annie really knew the way to a man's heart, he told himself with a wry smile before settling down to a relaxing evening, catching up with the latest news; this was followed by listening to his favourite music before turning in for the night.

The sun was just beginning to rise over the surrounding hills of the Wolds as Robert Laxton climbed reluctantly out of bed, stretched himself and checked the alarm clock that stood on the bedside cabinet, it was seven o'clock. After a shower and a shave he felt a new man. He had a strong feeling of well-being as he looked out at the sun rising over the castle ruins. He gave a deep sigh as he fastened his tie before making his way down the stairs. This was followed by a plate full of cereal and a couple of slices of toast before leaving the house and climbing into his car. Annie was just coming into the driveway as he started the engine. He gave her a wave as he drove out onto the lane. She returned the wave with a big smile as he drove off on the beginning of his journey to Lincoln, stopping on his way at Wragby to pick up his young partner.

'Good morning boss,' said Billings chirpily as he climbed into the car and fastened his seatbelt. Laxton nodded his head at him and smiled in return as he put the car into gear and accelerated away.

After half an hour had gone by and he had negotiated the heavy traffic, he drove into the police headquarters car park, after disembarking the two officers entered the police station.

Bellows welcomed them with the usual broad smile as they walked through reception to the chief's door; giving a quick knock they entered the office. The chief, seated behind his desk, greeted them with a nod as they sat down in the two chairs placed in front of him.

'I've had a reply regarding the phone numbers that were in the notebook,' he announced, looking at them over the rims of his glasses. There was a serious tone to his voice as he addressed them.

Pausing for a moment, he averted his eyes and looked down at the sheet of paper in front of him that had been forwarded to the office. He commenced reading out the addresses of the people involved:

'Allinson, 25 Lilac Street, Shiregreen, Sheffield, Yorkshire. Norwood, 6 Lancaster Drive, Hull, Yorkshire. Rostman, Westview, Croft Lane, Spalding, Lincolnshire. And of course, there are the Mallings.'

Wilberton leaned back in his seat and eyed the two officers sat in front of him, there was a deep frown on his forehead as he told them, 'We are going to have to tread warily as we go about investigating these people, I'm afraid they are going to find it hard to accept when we inform them that the children have been illegally adopted.'

He paused for a moment before stating that first of all he was going to contact the Allinsons, he reached out and picked up the phone.

Chapter 12

Michael Allinson, a six-foot handsome lad, leaned forward over the handlebars of his BSA motor cycle, his eyes were half closed, his long hair flowing back from his face as the wind whipped against it. He experienced a thrill every time the bike dipped as he negotiated the undulating hilly terrain that made up the countryside surrounding Sheffield, well known as the 'city of the seven hills'.

The motor bike, something he had always yearned for, had been a gift from his dad for his recent twentieth birthday.

'Michael I don't want you to go driving at speeds you can't cope with,' his dad had advised him when he took him to the dealers and told him to pick one from the array of shining new bikes. He plumped for the powerful BSA model with its chrome fittings. He smiled to himself as he drove carefully up the busy Bellhouse Road. A few minutes later he was parking up in the driveway of the semi-detached house on Lilac Street on what was known locally as the Flower Estate.

'I'm home Mum,' he called out as he opened the door and stepped into the hallway.

His mum, a worried expression on her lined face as she dried her hands on a towel, turned to him as he walked into the kitchen – she had a tear in her eye.

'Why are you looking so upset Mum?' he enquired, placing a comforting arm round her shoulder.

She chewed on her lip for a few seconds before telling him that when his dad came home she and his dad had something to tell him.

'He's just rung up and told me he will be home in about half an hour,' she told him in a quiet voice.

There was a questioning look on his face as he asked her, 'Is it serious?'

She shook her head and buried her face in her handkerchief, sobbing uncontrollably.

'Your dad will explain everything to you,' she told him, her voice muffled by the handkerchief.

After just over half an hour had gone by the front door opened; his dad, a heavily built man, walked into the kitchen, took his jacket off and sat down. He had a serious expression on his face as he addressed Michael.

'Now then lad,' he started in a broad Sheffield accent. 'Sit down I've got something to tell thee.'

He folded his arms and plucked at his bottom lip for a few seconds before telling the seated Michael, 'First of all let me say that your mum and I have loved you as if you were our own.'

Michael sat bolt upright in his seat as the implication of what his dad had said struck home.

'What do you mean Dad by, as if I was your own?' he queried, adding fervently: 'You are my mum and dad.'

His mum butted in. 'Tell him Arthur,' she said tearfully.

'All right Lilian, I am going to tell him,' rejoined her husband a little irritably, running his fingers through his thinning hair.

The young man was shaking his head, utterly baffled by what was being said.

'Tell me what?' he blurted.

Arthur held his hand up.

'First of all let me tell you that you were not born to us.'

'I... I don't understand,' gasped Michael, a questioning look on his face.

'What I mean is,' said Arthur, his brow furrowed, 'you were adopted.'

Michael sat back in his chair speechless. Lilian approached him, tears welling up in her blue eyes as she informed him that they chose him to be their son.

'What do you mean you chose me?' he queried, still baffled at the disclosure.

'Your mum and I...' Arthur paused for a moment as he indicated his wife before going on. 'Couldn't have children of our own. When we were told that you among other children were available we decided that we would go and see you before making up our minds.'

'We fell in love with you as soon as we set eyes on

you,' interrupted Lilian.

'Why are you telling me this now?' the young man enquired.

'We were informed today that we can expect a visit from the police,' intoned Arthur.

'A visit from the police?' repeated Michael, shaking his head from side to side. There was a look of disbelief on his face as he absorbed what he was being told by the ones he had always believed were his true parents.

'It seems that the people that we got you from may have acquired you illegally,' Arthur explained.

'What do you mean by illegally?'

'You may have been abducted from your rightful family,' declared Lilian, still dabbing her eyes.

'How were you chosen to adopt me?'

'We had to agree to pay ten thousand pounds over a period of time,' she told him.

'You mean to tell me you didn't suspect anything?' countered the young man.

Arthur looked down at the floor, his face reddening. 'We never thought…' he said lamely.

'Why didn't you adopt through the normal channels?'

'We tried over and over again but they turned us down,' explained Lilian, adding with a shrug of her shoulders: 'I don't know why.'

Michael sat for a few minutes mulling over in his mind the revelation that these two people, the ones he loved more than anyone else in the world, weren't his true mum and dad. He went over to Lilian, who was sobbing into her handkerchief; he had a concerned expression on his face.

'Never mind, as far as I'm concerned you are still my mum and dad, you've shown me a lot of love and affection and I love you both dearly,' he told them feelingly as he put his arm around Lilian's shoulders and gave her a hug.

After a long and uneventful drive from Lincoln, Inspector Laxton, accompanied by his partner Alan Billings, manoeuvred the car into the large car park outside police headquarters in the centre of Sheffield. Chief Inspector Wilberton, after an in-depth discussion over the phone with his counterpart in Sheffield had informed him that two of his officers would be coming to ask the couple who, it seems had unlawfully adopted a boy, a few questions. Climbing out of the car, Laxton and his young partner entered the imposing building.

'Good morning sir, can I help you?' enquired the tall lanky sergeant standing behind a long counter.

Laxton explained to him who they were and that they had arranged to see Chief Inspector Warren. The sergeant led them to a door at the back of the office, opening it he ushered them in, calling out, 'Inspector Laxton to see you sir.'

The chief came out from behind his desk to greet them as they entered the office, a broad smile on his face. After shaking hands with them he told them to take a seat.

'Now then Inspector,' he began, leaning his elbows on the desk in front of him before going on. 'Chief Inspector Wilberton has explained everything to me. I've been in touch with the Allinsons and they have agreed to talk to you.'

He paused for a few seconds to let the implication of what he was about to tell them sink in, before going on to explain that he wanted them to tread carefully as the Allinsons were under the impression that they hadn't broken any laws.

'I'm sending Police Sergeant Wilson to accompany you,' he told them.

Laxton nodded his head in acceptance as Warren reached out and picked up the phone. After speaking into for a few seconds, he turned to Laxton and told him, 'Sergeant Wilson will be with you shortly.'

After two or three minutes had gone by the door opened and a slim, smart, good looking policewoman came in – she had three stripes on her arm, it was Sergeant Barbara Wilson; after introducing them to her, the chief instructed her to assist the two officers as much as she could.

'I'll do that chief,' she assured him with a smile and a nod of her blonde head.

With this the three of them left the office and made their way to the car.

'Do you want to sit in one of the rear seats or in the passenger seat Sergeant?' enquired Laxton.

'I'll sit in the rear Inspector,' she replied as she opened the door and climbed in, exposing her stocking tops as she did so. Billings, who had reached out for the door in readiness to close it for her, quickly averted his eyes. She gave a half smile as she made herself comfortable.

'Now then Sergeant, I'll leave it to you to get us there!' exclaimed Laxton as they joined the heavy traffic.

Fifteen minutes later and after a few instructions they were leaving the busy city centre behind them. Another ten minutes and they were at the top of the steep Bellhouse Road and entering the Flower Estate.

'Take the next right,' the sergeant instructed him.

The name 'Lilac Street', was on the low wall as they slowly made their way along the street.

'Here we are,' stated the sergeant a little triumphantly as they reached number fifteen.

Piling out of the car they walked down the path that ran alongside the flower lined garden. Laxton smiled appreciatively as he ran his eyes over the garden. Although he wasn't much of a gardener himself, he did like to see a well-kept one. On reaching the door the sergeant rang the doorbell. A few seconds later the door opened to reveal a big well-built man in his fifties.

'Mr Arthur Allinson?' she enquired, a half smile on her face.

'Yes?' he replied as he ran his eyes over the three officers.

She explained to him that they would like to have a few words with him and his wife. He had a serious expression on his face as he invited them in and led them through the entrance hall and into a well-furnished lounge.

'I'll get the wife,' he told them as they each took a seat.

Laxton, who had chosen one of the plush easy chairs, ran his eyes round the room, taking in the portraits of local scenes that hung on the wall, as he waited for the man to bring his wife in. A couple of minutes went by before the man returned accompanied by a small slightly built woman.

'This is my wife Lilian,' he informed them on entering the room. The three officers got to their feet and shook the woman's hand; Lilian smiled and nodded her slightly greying head to each of them in turn, before taking a seat on the settee beside the police woman.

'Now then, what do you want to know?' asked Arthur, preferring to stand, his hands in his pockets.

Laxton leaned forward, his elbows on his knees and his hands clasped.

'First of all, you have a son?' he put to them, more a question than a statement.

The couple an expression of curiosity on their faces nodded their heads.

'We have,' they said in unison.

The inspector, his brow furrowed, looked down and clasped and unclasped his hands for a couple of seconds before adding in a somewhat solemn tone of voice, 'From the information that we have in our possession you say he is adopted.'

'Yes that's true,' they both rejoined.

He looked up into Arthur's brown eyes, telling him, 'There is no record in the files of your son being legally adopted.'

Allinson shuffled his feet, there was a rasping sound as he took his hands out of his pockets and scratched his unshaven chin nervously.

'We've got proof that we adopted him,' interrupted Lilian, jumping to her feet and going over to a drawer in the glass fronted cabinet; sliding it open she took out an envelope and passed it to Laxton. Opening the envelope he took out a sheet of paper stating that they had paid in full the amount of ten thousand pounds for the adoption of the boy.

Laxton pursed his lips as he studied the document, before raising his head and looking the woman in the eyes, telling her, 'I'm afraid this isn't proof of a legal adoption.'

At that moment a young man burst into the room. He had overheard the comments alluding to his adoption. He looked down at Laxton.

'Why are you asking questions about my adoption?' he asked sharply.

The inspector sat up in his seat and addressed the young man. 'I'm trying to find out whether your adoption was legal,' he explained.

Arthur Allinson butted in. 'This is Michael our adopted son,' he said a little aggressively.

'That Mr Allinson is what we are attempting to discover,' Laxton put to him, before turning back to the young man and informing him: 'Michael, we have acquired certain details that point to the fact that you may have been abducted when you were three and a half years old.'

Michael Allinson, his young brow deeply furrowed, ran his fingers through his thick mop of black hair as he told the inspector, 'I don't care what the circumstances are, I love my parents,' he said, his voice full of feeling as he walked across the room and stood between Arthur and Lilian Allinson, placing his arms round their shoulders affectionately.

Sergeant Barbara Wilson spoke up, addressing the young man. 'We need to discover who your natural parents are Michael,' she told him in a friendly tone of voice before going on to explain to him: 'If it is proved that you have been illegally abducted, then the people who are involved have broken the law and must be punished.'

'What will happen to us?' enquired Lilian, a little tearfully.

'That, I don't know,' replied the sergeant, adding in a solemn tone of voice: 'I would imagine that the fact that you have given Michael a good life would go down well with any court.'

'Where do we go from here?' enquired Arthur, a worried expression on his face.

'For the moment we'll leave things as they are,' grunted Laxton as he got to his feet in readiness to leave; his two companions following suit. He was just about to go through the door when he turned and addressed Michael. 'Do you have any birth marks or scars from when you were a child?' he asked him.

The young man scratched the back of his head before telling him that he had a slightly deformed left foot. Laxton had a questioning look on his face.

'In what way do you mean, "deformed"?' he enquired.

Michael took both his shoes and socks off and stood with his feet together. His left foot was a good inch smaller than his right. Laxton nodded his head.

'That should be good enough,' he told the young man.

'Why do you want to know?' enquired Michael as he pulled on his socks; he had a puzzled expression on his face.

The inspector was silent for a few seconds before looking him in the eyes and informing him that the information would be necessary for future reference regarding the identity of his true parents.

'Does that mean I will get to meet them?' asked Michael.

Laxton nodded his head, telling him, 'Yes, that is of course if all the evidence that we have collated matches up.'

With this he went through the door followed by his two companions.

'It looks as though we have made some progress,' stated the sergeant as she made herself comfortable in the rear seat.

'I agree,' rejoined the inspector, adding philosophically as he turned the key in the ignition: 'But there is a lot of water to go under the bridge yet.'

Twenty minutes later they dropped the sergeant off at police headquarters, before carrying on with their journey back to Lincoln.

'By the way, I almost forgot, Mum has asked me to tell you that she would like us to have lunch with her and Dad,' Billings put to the inspector.

Laxton looked at his watch, it was eleven o'clock.

'Did she say when she wants us to be there?' he asked his partner as he changed into top gear.

'No, but she usually has it ready for around one o'clock,' Billings told him with a shrug of his shoulders.

'We should just about make it,' rejoined the inspector.

An hour later they arrived at Lincoln headquarters; climbing out of the car they made their way across the car park and through the main doors. Sergeant

Bellows gave them a nod as they walked through on their way to the chief's office. Wilberton was sat behind his desk waiting for them as they walked through the door, his hands clasped in front of him as the two officers seated themselves in two seats opposite him.

'What have you come up with?' he enquired, a questioning expression on his face.

Laxton went through all the details that they had gleaned from their interview with the Allinsons.

The chief stroked his chin as he mulled over what he had been told.

'So we now know that the Allinsons do have a child which they have admitted was adopted by them,' he muttered, adding: 'If the deformity in his foot that the boy has shown you is duplicated by a similar statement from the Batleys, then we have a match. I'll get in touch with Market Rasen police department and ask them to have a word with the Batleys.'

He picked up the phone and dialled a number.

'Hello can I speak to the officer in charge of the Market Rasen police station?'

He nodded his head at the receiver as he listened to the reply. After giving the address of the Batleys, he asked the officer, 'Can you get in touch with them?' before going on to explain to him that he wanted confirmation of a match between the young man that the Allinsons say they adopted and the boy that was abducted from the Batleys. He then went on to describe the deformity in the foot of Michael Allinson. If the Batley boy had the same deformity then it was almost certain that they were one and the same.

'Leave it with me, I'll get on to it right away, as soon as it is confirmed I'll get back on to you,' the officer at the other end of the phone assured him.

Wilberton put the phone back on its rest and turned to Laxton, telling him, 'I've had a phone call from Inspector Jenkins, they have arrested the man named Ronald Miller for questioning.' He paused for a moment before going on to tell him that the man named Finchley had informed the police when Miller arrived back in his lodgings.

'I want you to go to Nottingham again and see what you can find out regarding Miller's connection with the abductions,' Wilberton instructed them.

'We'll get down there right after we've had something to eat, Chief,' rejoined Laxton, getting to his feet.

Checking his watch, he turned to Billings after handing him the car keys.

'We've got twenty minutes to get to Wragby Alan. You will have to put your foot down, I don't want to upset your mum,' he told his young partner, with a shake of his head.

Taking their leave, the two left the building and quickly climbed into the car. Twenty minutes later they arrived at the Billings' home to be greeted with Alan's smiling mum.

'That's what I call timing,' she chuckled as they walked through the door.

Half an hour later after thanking Alan's mum for the excellent meal of steak and chips followed by home-made apple pie, the satisfied, well-fed pair went on their way.

Apart from being hampered by the numerous

heavy goods vehicles the journey to Nottingham was uneventful. After making their way through the busy city centre they arrived at police headquarters. Chief Inspector Warren was waiting for them as they entered his office. He greeted them with the obligatory smile and the shaking of hands before telling the inspector that they had Ronald Miller in custody.

'I would just like to question him regarding his connection with the children who were abducted,' Laxton informed him.

Warren went to the door, opened it and called out to the sergeant in reception.

The sergeant entered the office.

'Yes Chief,' he said inquiringly.

'Can you bring Ronald Miller to the interrogation room right away Sergeant?' he told him.

Laxton and Billings followed the chief out of the office to a sparsely furnished room at the rear of the police station. After a couple of minutes' wait the sergeant entered the room accompanied by a tall, heavily built man, who looked to be in his late fifties. The chief who was sat behind a desk, indicated for him to take a seat in front of him.

'What this all about and why am I being kept here?' he snapped, his unshaven chin jutting out belligerently.

The chief inspector, ignoring Miller's attitude, addressed him; he had a serious expression on his face as he did so.

'It has come to our notice that you may have had some involvement in the abduction of children who went missing in nineteen sixty-eight,' he put to him.

The man's dark brown eyes narrowed as he took in the implication of what the chief was saying, he shook his head slowly from side to side as he refuted what was being stated.

'I've had nothing to do with the abduction of children,' he blustered, his face reddening.

'What is your connection with a Martin Fulbek?' Laxton put to him.

'I don't know any Martin Fulbek,' he grated, again shaking his head.

There was a lull in the questioning for a spell, then Chief Inspector Warren leaned forward and looked Miller in the eyes before informing him, his voice dropping in volume, 'Mr Finchley, the man who runs the lodgings where you were staying has told us that you brought Martin Fulbek to stay overnight at the lodging house.'

Miller's eyes went from side to side as if he was looking for a way out.

'Okay, so I knew him,' he snapped. 'That doesn't mean anything.'

'Ahh but it does!' exclaimed the chief, meaningfully, before going on to add: 'We have interviewed Martin Fulbek's wife; she has admitted to us that she and her husband had four children in their care. She told us that the children were to stay with them until suitable couples were found to adopt them.' He paused for a moment then went on to say, 'She has also told us the names of the people who have adopted them.'

The man they were questioning straightened up, ran his fingers through his wiry greying hair and took a deep breath then breathed out slowly, his shoulders sagging as he did so; he had the look of a beaten man.

'Okay,' he muttered giving a shrug of his broad shoulders. 'What do you want to know?'

Laxton took up the questioning.

'Do you recall the names, Malling, Norwood, Rothman and Allinson?'

Miller ran his fingers up and down the bridge of his nose as he cast his mind back.

'As far as I can remember they are the names of the persons who adopted the children,' he muttered.

'Were you responsible for the abduction of these children at the time they went missing?' enquired Laxton, leaning forward, his elbows on his knees.

Miller clasped his hands and gazed down at his shoes for a couple of seconds before answering.

'I wasn't personally responsible for picking up the children. My job was to find suitable couples to adopt them.'

'What do you mean by "suitable"?' enquired the chief, butting in.

'We wanted to make sure that the children were properly cared for,' rejoined Miller with a shrug of his shoulders.

'If you were so caring, why did you take the children in the first place?' the chief put to him.

The beaten man clasped and unclasped his hands before answering.

'Money,' he declared bluntly, looking the chief in the eyes.

Warren shook his head in disbelief as he asked him, 'Do you mean to tell me that you would ruin the parents of these children's lives for money?'

There was no reply.

'You said we. Does that mean that there were others involved?' Laxton put to him.

Miller, who had been looking down at the floor suddenly directed his gaze at the inspector, his eyes hardening as he told him adamantly, 'I'm saying no more.'

Laxton sat back in his chair and folded his arms; after a few seconds contemplating the sharp reply, he leaned forward, his elbows on his knees.

'Mr Miller you are in no position to refuse to help us with our inquiries,' he put to him, adding, his voice dropping in volume: 'We already have enough on you, taking into consideration the facts that you have already admitted to. It will be to your advantage if you help us.'

Miller closed his eyes and clenched his fists; it was obvious that he was beginning to realise the seriousness of the situation he was in. After a few seconds had gone by he opened his eyes and visibly relaxed.

'Okay, I'll help you as much as I can.'

His reply had the air of a beaten man.

At that moment a young constable came into the room carrying a tray with four mugs of coffee on it; after they had taken one each from the tray they thanked the constable, who then left the room. Laxton took a drink of his coffee before turning to Miller again; he informed him that they had already contacted Mrs Watlng and Mr and Mrs Allinson before adding, 'I would like you to verify the addresses of the other two couples, the Norwoods and the Rothmans.'

Miller reached into his pocket, took out his wallet and extracted a folded piece of paper. Opening it he read out, 'William and Jane Rothman, West View, Croft Lane, Spalding.'

He paused for a moment to finish his coffee before going on.

'John and Margaret Norwood, six Lancaster Drive, Hull.'

Laxton nodded his head.

'Those are the names and addresses that we've got,' he told Warren, a note of satisfaction in his voice as he turned his attention back to Miller.

'Now then Mr Miller, all we want to know from you is the name and address of the others that are involved in the organisation and instigation of the abductions.'

Miller, his eyes slits, stroked his chin nervously; the consequences of disclosing the name of his accomplice, was giving him cause for concern. Suddenly he made his mind up. After taking a deep breath he told them that the name of the man who was involved with him was a Thomas Wooding.

Billings, who had been assiduously writing down the facts in his notebook, piped up.

'What's his address?'

The by now sweating man told him, with a weary air of resignation that Wooding's address was Westrel House, Chapel Lane, Narborough, Norfolk.

'If I remember right, Narborough is a village about eight miles from RAF Marham,' said Laxton. He had a nostalgic expression on his face as he cast his mind back. 'I was stationed in the RAF near there for a while; it's right out in the sticks.'

'I'll get in touch with Kings Lynn police headquarters and have him placed in custody,' the chief announced.

Laxton looked at his watch – it was four o'clock. He got to his feet and turned to Warren.

'That should just about do us for today Chief,' he declared.

Chief Inspector Warren nodded his head in agreement as a dejected Miller was led away.

Laxton thanked the chief for his input before he and Billings left the building and walked across the car park to the car. Handing the car keys to his partner he climbed into the passenger seat. A few minutes later they were wending their way through the heavy traffic as they made their way out of the city centre; after another twenty minutes they were on the A46 and on their way to Lincoln. After an uneventful journey they eventually pulled into the Lincoln headquarters car park. Laxton checked his watch as they climbed out of the car and went into Wilberton's office. It was five fifteen. The chief looked up at them over the rim of his glasses as the two officers entered the office and took a seat.

'What have you come up with Robert?' he enquired as they made themselves comfortable.

Laxton turned to Billings.

'Can you give the chief the information that you've written down Alan?' he told the young man.

Billings jumped to his feet and handed his notebook with the information that he had jotted down during the interview with Miller.

'Mmm,' muttered Wilberton as he slowly absorbed the information. 'It looks as though we've got them all bang to rights.'

Laxton nodded his head in agreement before telling the chief, 'We'll see what progress we can make tomorrow,'

'I think it would be a good idea for you to start with a visit to the families that have taken in two of the children that were abducted,' the chief advised him, before going on to suggest that they could start with the Rostmans who lived in Spalding.

'We'll do that chief,' Laxton rejoined, putting his hands on his knees and preparing to rise.

He gave a nod at Wilberton as he turned to leave the office with Billings following him out of the door before making their way to the car.

'I reckon we've really achieved something today Alan,' he remarked, a hint of satisfaction in his voice as he climbed into the car and fastening his seatbelt.

'Let's hope we have the same success tomorrow boss,' rejoined Billings as he followed suit and clipped his seatbelt into place; Laxton started the car and drove out of the car park. A black cloud was just beginning to cover the sun which was low in the sky as he dropped Billings off at his home in Wragby.

After a farewell wave and a, 'See you tomorrow,' Laxton set off for home. He checked his watch as he turned off the main road to take the lane that led to Old Bolingbroke. It was six thirty.

He smiled ruefully as he told himself that he had been working overtime; ten minutes later he arrived at his cottage. Horatio was there to greet him with a loud meow as he walked across the yard and opened the back door, followed closely by the cat.

'Okay, okay! I've got the message,' he exclaimed, a

smile on his face as he went to the fridge, took out a smelly plate of sardines and placed it on the floor, as a hungry Horatio unceremoniously pushed his hand out of the way to get at it.

Going into the dining room, he picked up a note on the table telling him, 'Dinner in the oven, don't let it go cold.' It was signed 'Annie'.

He shook his head and smiled as he opened the oven, took out the appetising meal of two lamb chops, potatoes and veg and placed it on the table. After opening a can of Guinness, he sat down at the table.

'Good old Annie,' he muttered, his mouth full as he tucked in.

After taking a shower he decided that as tomorrow would be busy, he would have an early night.

Chapter 13

Laxton, after a good night's rest, felt great as he finished his breakfast and made his way out of his cottage in Old Bolingbroke, a row of larch trees that were growing along the side of a field in the distance were leaning over as the strong blustery wind pushed against them getting into his car he drove out on to the lane. It was just beginning to spit with rain as he exited the village and made his way up the steep country lane that led to the main road. Around forty minutes later he arrived at Wragby; Alan was waiting for him. He was standing in the doorway of the house sheltering from the rain, which was by now beginning to come down heavily, as the inspector arrived. He made a quick dash to the car and jumped in.

'Morning boss,' he said as he fastened his seatbelt.

Laxton nodded his head in reply as he engaged the gear and drove away. He took his hand off the steering wheel and checked his watch; it was eight thirty.

'We should reach Spalding around nine thirty,' he muttered as he kept one eye on the road.

A few minutes later they were clear of Wragby and were eating up the miles.

They headed first for Sleaford and then on to Spalding. Laxton was deep in thought, his brain working overtime going over the events of the past few days as he drove along, the wipers swishing from side to side as they fought to clear the by now torrential rain, making the what was usually a pleasant journey through the open countryside, into a dismal one, as they splashed through deep puddles of water.

'Here we are,' announced Laxton with a sigh of relief, as they approached a sign with the name 'Spalding' on it. He slowed down as he drove through the almost deserted town.

Billings took out a handkerchief and rubbed it across the misted side window to clear it as he watched out for Croft Lane, to no avail. The inspector stopped the car and turned to Billings telling him, 'We'll have to ask someone where it is Alan.'

At that moment an elderly woman with an umbrella was walking briskly towards them; as she drew level with the car Billings, who had wound down the window, called out loudly, 'Excuse me missus!'

The woman stopped and walked over the grass verge to the car.

'Yes?' she said, a questioning expression on her face as she addressed the young man.

'Can you direct us to Croft Lane please?'

'Mmm, Croft Lane,' she muttered, her face almost obscured by the big umbrella. 'Now let me see. Ah yes I remember now.'

Pointing along the road she told him, 'If you carry

on along this road for about two hundred yards you'll come to Drew Lane, turn down there and you will come eventually to Croft Lane.'

Billings thanked her as she turned and squelched across the grass as she continued on her way.

Laxton carried on for the two hundred yards that the woman had indicated and came to Drew Lane; turning down it he drove for about a quarter of a mile, passing old country cottages before coming to Croft Lane. He gave a sigh of relief as he turned down the lane. He noted with some trepidation the large holes in the surface filled with rainwater which was still bucketing down from a grey sky. They had travelled about fifty yards when Billings announced, 'Here we are boss.' The sign, 'West View', stood at the front of the drive of, what looked like an old dilapidated cottage.

Laxton stopped the car and they both climbed out and splashed their way to the front door which had an old iron doorknocker. Billings lifted it and gave a loud knock. The sound of a dog barking came from inside the cottage; footsteps could be heard approaching the door. A few seconds later the door opened to reveal a well-built woman wearing thick rimmed glasses, she looked to be in her late fifties.

'Mrs Jane Rostman?' asked the inspector politely.

She nodded her head, a questioning crease on her brow.

'Who wants to know?' she enquired a little sharply, as she pushed back a frond of greying hair that had fallen over her eyes.

Laxton explained to her that they were police officers making enquiries.

'You'd better come inside out of the rain before you catch pneumonia,' she told them a little sharply, as she opened the door wide.

They followed her along a somewhat dark hallway into the back kitchen. The top of a man's bald head was sticking up over the back of an armchair. He sat up, turned round and looked at them as they came through the door. He greeted them with a smile and a nod of his head.

'My husband William,' she told them.

The two officers returned his nod as they were invited to take a seat.

'Would you like a cup of tea?' she asked them as they were making themselves comfortable.

They both declined, telling her that they would only be a few minutes.

'What do you want to know?' she asked, as she took a seat opposite them.

'We are making enquiries about an adopted child, er, a girl,' Laxton put to her.

'I don't understand,' the woman said, shaking her head, there was a confused expression on her face.

'We have been informed that you have an adopted daughter,' he put to her as delicately as he could before going on to ask her if it would be possible to have a word with the girl.

The woman looked down at her clasped hands, a wistful expression on her face.

'I'm afraid you can't,' she said, almost in a whisper.

'Why not?' enquired the inspector, his brow furrowed questioningly.

William got to his feet, went over to his wife and

sat on the arm of her chair before placing his arm around her shoulders.

'Don't get upset dear,' he told her comfortingly.

Laxton shook his head slowly from side to side; there was a perplexed expression on his face.

'I don't understand!' he exclaimed.

Jane looked at him, her eyes brimming with tears.

'Margaret isn't with us anymore,' she told the inspector as she took her glasses off and dabbed her eyes with a handkerchief that William had given her.

'Where is she?' asked Laxton.

William, who was still sitting on the arm of the easy chair, got to his feet and stood for a few seconds facing Laxton. Taking a deep breath, he looked down at the seated inspector and told him, his voice dropping in volume, 'She passed away just over eight years ago.'

Laxton exchanged glances with Billings before turning his attention back to the couple, a serious expression on his face.

'How did this happen?' he queried.

'She became listless and had no energy. We thought she needed a tonic,' she muttered, almost under her breath. William reached down and squeezed her shoulder to comfort her. He continued with the account of what happened.

'We took her to see the doctor, thinking a few tablets would put her right.' He stopped and gave a shrug of his shoulders before going on to say, 'We didn't know that she was seriously ill.'

'What was she suffering from?' Laxton put to him bluntly.

'The specialist told us that it was leukaemia.' He paused for a moment before adding in a quiet voice, 'She was dead in six months.'

'I know that it has been painful to go through what has happened to the girl Mr Rostman. But I must tell you that the means by which you came to adopt her were unlawful.'

'We were told that Jane's parents had died and as we couldn't have children of our own we adopted her,' was the reply from Mrs Rostman, butting in.

'That may be so my dear,' said the inspector, softening his voice, 'but the truth is she was abducted from her true parents.'

The couple exchanged looks of horror as they took in what the inspector had just told them.

'We had no idea,' they said in unison, shaking their heads.

'Well the best I can do is report what you have told me and it will be up to the powers that be to make a decision,' he informed them.

'Does that mean that we will be charged?' enquired Jane worriedly.

The inspector shrugged his shoulders before telling them, 'Owing to the fact that you gave her a good, happy home during the time that she lived with you, should influence the authorities.'

He got to his feet and was just about to leave when he turned and addressed them, 'Did the girl ever tell you her name?'

'Well, when she first came here, she did tell us that her name was Jane Benning.' She went quiet for a few seconds before adding, 'We decided that we would name her Margaret.'

After assuring them that he didn't think that they would have a lot to worry about, he and his partner left.

Laxton checked his watch, it was ten forty-five; he turned to Billings as they walked up the garden path to the car. 'You drive Alan,' he told him, handing him the keys.

The rain was beginning to abate as they approached Sleaford. Billings took his eyes off the road for a second as he addressed the inspector.

'Do you really think that they might get off lightly?' he put to him.

'I don't see why not,' declared Laxton with a shake of his head. 'They've shown a lot of love and care for the girl and there's also the fact that they didn't know that she had been abducted.'

Another hour went by; the rain had stopped and the sun was beginning to show through the clouds as they approached Lincoln police station. After parking the car, Laxton and Billings went inside to report to the chief inspector. Wilberton greeted them with a nod of his head as they entered his office.

'What have you come up with Robert?' he asked the inspector as the two officers took a seat in front of him.

Laxton, his hands clasped in front of him, proceeded to go through all the details of their interview with the Rostmans. Wilberton, who had been listening intently, sat back in his chair deep in thought; after a while he looked at the inspector over the rims of his glasses and addressed him.

'It's going to come as quite a shock when the

parents of this girl find out that she has passed away,' he declared somewhat morosely.

'What are we going to do about the Rostmans Chief?' enquired Laxton.

'What do you mean?' rejoined Wilberton.

'Will they be charged with aiding and abetting?'

Wilberton reached up, took his glasses off and breathed on the lenses then commenced polishing them with one of the small sheets of tissue that were in a box in front of him as he thought over what Laxton had put to him; after a few seconds he dropped the tissue into the waste paper basket that stood on the floor beside the desk before turning to the inspector.

'I can't see that happening Robert,' he told him as he put his glasses back on. 'They have said that they didn't know that the girl had been abducted; if they can convince the authorities of that they will probably be let off lightly.'

Laxton nodded his head in agreement.

'Now then Robert,' said the chief in a more business-like manner. 'I want you to get in touch with the Norwoods in Hull and look into their involvement with the abducted children.'

'We'll get over there after lunch,' the inspector assured him.

He looked at his watch; it was twelve forty-five. His face was grim as he announced, 'We'll have to get in touch with the Bennings and give them the bad news,'

'I'll see to that Robert,' the chief rejoined as Laxton and his partner turned to leave.

'We'll get a meal at the restaurant round the corner,' suggested the inspector. 'It's only around ten minutes' walk.'

Striding out, the two officers arrived at the restaurant-cum-chip shop some nine minutes later. After a satisfying meal of haddock and chips washed down with a mug of coffee, they returned to the car and set off on the journey to Hull. The sun was reflecting off the wide stretch of water as they crossed over the Humber Bridge and eventually arriving at Kingston upon Hull.

Lancaster Drive was situated on the outskirts of the city; After searching for some twenty minutes they finally came across it. Laxton slowed down as they watched out for number six.

'Here we are,' declared Billings, pointing his finger at a detached house that stood back from the road, a nearly new Volvo stood in the driveway.

Laxton nodded his head as he stopped the car at the front of the house; climbing out, he and Billings opened the front gate and walked along the path which led through a well-tended garden which Laxton looked at with appreciation as they approached the front door. Billings rang the doorbell. The inspector chewed on his bottom lip as he waited for someone to answer it. After a minute or so the door opened. A good looking young woman who looked to be about twenty years old stood looking at him.

'Yes can I help you?' she enquired politely, a smile on her face.

Laxton, returning her smile, enquired, 'Are Mr and Mrs Norwood in?'

The young woman, a questioning expression on

her face, asked, 'Who are you?'

Laxton explained to her that they were police officers and that they would like to have a word with them.

'Well I'm afraid you can't at the moment, they are not in,' she told him politely.

'Have you any idea how long will they be?' he enquired.

'Well I don't think they will be long,' she said with a shake of her head, her golden locks swishing from side to side as she did so. 'They've gone shopping,' she told them.

The inspector stroked his chin for a couple of seconds as he contemplated his next move.

'You can come in and wait,' she offered.

'Thank you that's very kind of you,' he replied in a soft voice, as he and Billings stepped into the hallway.

'You can sit in here,' she told them as she led them into a large well-furnished lounge.

Thanking her they seated themselves in the two armchairs as she left them alone. Laxton looked around the comfortably furnished room; his eyes settling on the two watercolour paintings that were hanging on the walls.

'Would you like a drink?' a voice trilled from the kitchen.

'Yes please,' they rejoined loudly.

'Coffee or tea?'

'Er, coffee please.'

A few minutes later she came back in the room carrying a tray with three cups, a spoon and a small bowl of sugar on it. Placing the tray on a small table in front of them, she sat down on the settee. They both nodded their thanks as they reached out and took a coffee each, Laxton shaking his head as she offered the sugar to him; his partner had no such inhibitions as he scooped two heaped spoons and dropped them in his drink. The inspector was just about to lift his cup to his lips when there was a loud bump and the front door burst open.

'Ahh that must be Mum and Dad now!' exclaimed the young woman, getting to her feet as a middle aged couple came through the door carrying bags of shopping.

Marjory Norwood looked at the two men who had jumped to their feet as they entered; there was a questioning frown on her forehead as she placed the two large plastic bags that she was carrying on the floor.

'Mr and Mrs Norwood?' enquired the inspector as he stepped forward, a smile on his face.

The couple, who looked to be in their sixties, nodded their heads in assent.

'And who might you be?' was the somewhat surly response from the overweight, six-foot, grey-haired man standing in front of them.

Laxton coughed into his hand to clear his throat before going on to inform them that they were police officers.

'Police officers!' they exclaimed in unison. 'What do you want with us?'

'We are here to ask you a few questions regarding your adopted daughter,'

'Our adopted daughter?' retorted Arthur Norwood sharply, adding, 'I, I don't know what you are talking about.'

Laxton looked the man straight in the eyes, giving him a long probing look. He knew instantly that he wasn't telling the truth.

'Mr Norwood I think you do,' he replied, a little acidly, as the red faced man in front of him quickly looked away.

'What is it you want to know?' the frail Marjory Norwood put to the inspector, in a more conciliatory tone of voice.

'We just need to ask you a few questions regarding the daughter that you adopted,' said Laxton, repeating the request.

At that moment the young woman jumped to her feet and addressed the inspector.

'As I'm the only daughter I presume you are referring to me.'

Marjory Norwood stepped between the inspector and her daughter.

'Yes Caroline, he is referring to you,' she told the young woman a little apologetically.

'I, I don't understand Mum,' she said falteringly.

Marjory Norwood took her daughter by the shoulders, sat her down on the settee and looked into her eyes.

'We should have told you a long time ago Caroline.' She paused for a few seconds, tears welling up in her eyes as she explained to her with a shake of her head, 'We were afraid that you might lose your feelings for us.'

The young woman sat with her hands clasped in her lap for a while as she mulled over in her mind the implication of her words. Reaching out, she placed her arms round her mum's shoulders before laying her greying head on her breast as she confided in a soft voice, 'Whatever the outcome, you've been good parents to me and as far as I'm concerned you are my mum and dad and I love you both dearly.'

Then she turned to the inspector, her brow creased questioningly.

'Are my true mum and dad still alive?'

Laxton nodded his head. 'They are,' he assured her.

'Will I be able to see them?'

'I reckon so, er, eventually.'

'What do you mean by eventually?'

'Well I should think it will be when we can get you all together.'

'All,' she repeated. 'Are there more?'

'I'm afraid so,' the inspector told her with a nod of his head.

'Did my parents give me up for adoption?' she put to him, a serious expression on her face.

'No, they were broken hearted when they lost you.'

'Did the authorities take me away from them?' she persisted.

Laxton didn't answer; he turned away from her and addressed Arthur Norwood. 'By the way, did you know the name of Caroline's family?'

'Why do you want to know?' snapped Norwood.

Laxton let the man's snotty attitude go, getting annoyed wouldn't help.

'The children that were abducted have to be matched up with their parents,' he explained.

'When she first came to us she told us that her name was Caroline Gateland, we decided to keep the same Christian name,' rejoined Arthur.

Caroline butted in. 'You are saying that I was abducted.' It was more a question than a statement.

Laxton gave a nod of his head as he told her, 'That's so.'

'We didn't abduct her,' interrupted Marjory, shaking her head vigorously.

The inspector held his hand up.

'I know you weren't responsible for her going missing, but I would like to know how you came by her,' he countered.

She and her husband exchanged glances; he gave her a meaningful look. Ignoring him she pushed a tendril of greying hair back from over her eyes and turned to the inspector.

'We couldn't have children owing to me having to have a hysterectomy. Arthur was coming up against problems finding a job.' She paused for a moment to clear her throat before carrying on. 'The powers that be told us that we didn't pass the test and were refused permission to adopt a child through the normal channels. Arthur's great aunt had passed away and left him twenty-five thousand pounds in her will. We were contacted by a man named Miller who told us that he would put our name forward to be given the chance of adopting a child. He told us that it would cost us ten thousand pounds. After giving the proposition a lot of thought, we decided to go along with it. Two weeks later we were blessed with our Caroline.'

She turned and gave the young woman at her side a hug.

'Didn't you see the incidents of children being abducted in the papers?'

Laxton had a look of incredulity in his eyes as he asked the question.

She shook her head.

'We never buy papers do we Arthur?'

Her husband shook his head.

'No, we didn't know anything like that was going on.'

Laxton stood for a few seconds in silence before turning to Billings, who had been listening carefully to what was being said and jotting it down in his notebook.

'I reckon that's just about it for now Alan,' he said as he turned to leave.

'What happens now inspector?' asked Caroline.

'You will probably be introduced to your true parents in the near future. We will contact you to let you know when that will be,' he explained as he and his partner left the room.

After wishing the family goodbye they exited the property and went to the car. Laxton paused for a moment, just as he was about to open the car door; he glanced up at the heavy clouds that were forming in the sky. He gave a slight shake of his head.

'Looks like rain,' he mumbled under his breath, as he climbed in the car and fastened his seatbelt.

After making himself comfortable, he turned to his young partner. 'Well that's been a real eye opener!' he exclaimed.

Alan, who was driving, nodded his head in agreement as he engaged the gear and drove off; there was a heavy mist hanging over the Humber and it was beginning to spit with rain as they negotiated the long bridge that spanned it, an hour later they arrived back at headquarters.

Wilberton was in his usual place, behind his desk as they entered his office. After instructing Bellows to send in three coffees he turned to the inspector, who with his partner had taken a seat.

'How did it go?'

Laxton went on to brief him on the afternoon's events; the chief, leaning forward, placed his elbows on the desk in front of him and formed a pyramid with his fingers as he listened intently to the detailed account.

'Mmm it seems that they are another couple who have made a happy home for the girl they adopted, even though it was illegal,' he intoned, a thoughtful expression on his face.

At that moment WPC Smithson, a new addition to Sergeant Bellows' staff came in with the three coffees on a tray. Wilberton sat back in his seat as she placed the tray on the desk in front of him. The young blonde-haired woman smiled as she turned to leave; the three men giving her a nod of thanks, as she withdrew, each of them picking up a cup of coffee. After taking a sip, the chief turned to the subject in hand.

'I've received a phone call from Kings Lynn informing me that they have apprehended Thomas Wooding. After discovering that he had been 'shopped' by Miller, he admitted his involvement in the abductions. They also picked up Martin Fulbek;

he was staying at the same address.'

He reached out, picked up his coffee and took another drink before going on.

'It seems that Wooding and Miller devised a plot between them in which they went round different areas with the sole purpose of picking up very young children and placed them in the care of Martin and Janet Fulbek. The children were then given to couples who were desperate to adopt a child, for a fee of ten thousand pounds. These couples, for one reason or another could not get permission to adopt a child through the normal channels.'

Pausing for a couple of seconds, he reached out, picked up the phone and dialled a number.

The phone rang, Arthur Norwood picked up the receiver. 'Hello, Arthur Norwood speaking.'

The voice on the other end informed him that they were the police and that they would like Mr Arthur and Mrs Marjory Norwood to go to Lincoln police headquarters on Wednesday the 25th of May at two o'clock, in connection with the adoption of their daughter Caroline.

Arthur Norwood nodded his head at the receiver.

'Okay,' he told the person on the other end of the phone. 'We'll be there.'

'Who was that?' enquired his wife Marjory.

He explained to her as he put the phone down, that it was a call from the Lincoln police asking them to be at the station on Monday at two o'clock.

'What do they want?'

He gave a shrug of his shoulders before telling her

that it was in connection with their adoption of Caroline. His wife's hand went to her mouth.

'Do you think we will be in trouble?' she enquired nervously.

'I don't think so,' he told her with a shake of his head.

'We haven't broken any laws,' he assured her.

At that moment, Caroline came through the door.

'What's the matter Mum?' she asked, a questioning expression on her face.

Marjory explained to her that the police had wanted to interview them regarding her adoption. Caroline reached out, placed her arm round her mum's shoulder and gave her a comforting hug. 'Don't worry, I'll stand by you,' she whispered in her mum's ear, feelingly.

Lilian Allinson was hanging her washing on the line when her son William called out loudly, 'Mum you are wanted on the phone.'

'Coming,' she replied with some difficulty, the peg in her mouth hindering her. Taking it out, she finished fastening a towel on the line before making her way into the house and picking up the phone. The voice on the other end informed her that it was the police and that they wanted her to go to Lincoln police headquarters on Monday the 25th at two o'clock. She was told that it was to do with their adoption of Michael.

'All right we'll be there,' she replied hesitantly.

Half an hour later her husband Arthur walked through the door; she told him of the phone call.

'What do you think they want us there for Arthur?'

He gave a shrug of his shoulders, telling her, 'It could be anything. Anyway I don't think we have anything to worry about.'

His reply didn't sound very convincing.

Wilberton put the phone down and turned to Laxton, who had been sat in silence as the chief made the phone calls.

'I've already been in touch with the Gatelands and the Batleys, telling them to be here on Monday. We'll see what transpires.'

Laxton checked his watch; it was five thirty. He addressed his young partner. 'Time we weren't here Alan,' he confided, placing his hands on his knees and getting to his feet.

'See you on Monday Chief,' he announced, giving a farewell wave of his hand as he left the office closely followed by Billings. Wilberton, who had turned his attention to some paper work, glanced up at the two officers over the rim of his glasses, acknowledging them with a nod of his head.

The rain had abated a little as they approached Wragby. A few minutes later Laxton stopped the car outside his partner's home; Billings jumped out.

'See you boss,' he called out cockily, as he slammed the car door and broke into a run through the light rain.

Laxton gave a farewell wave of his hand before driving off, a wry smile on his face.

The rain had stopped and the sun, which was low in the sky, was just beginning to show through the light cloud as he pulled into his driveway. Taking a deep breath of the late evening fresh country air, he made his way to the back door of his cottage.

'The village of Old Bolingbroke really is something special in the quiet of the evening,' he told himself, a contented feeling coming over him, as he took his jacket off and hung it in the clothes closet in the hallway. Annie was bent over taking his dinner out of the oven, her broad rump sticking out.

'Don't you dare,' she told him laughingly, as he raised his hand, a broad smile on his face.

'Annie that looks fit for a king,' he chuckled, eyeing the large plate of stew and dumplings as he went to the fridge, took out a bottle of beer before tucking in.

'I'll be off now Mr Laxton,' she announced, her eyes still twinkling as she left.

Chapter 14

It was eight o'clock Monday morning; Robert Laxton placed a dish of cat food on the floor for Horatio, who was meowing as he circled around his master's feet.

'There you are m'lad,' muttered the inspector as the cat pushed his hand out of the way in his eagerness to get at the smelly food.

There was a smile on his face as he went out of the door and made his way to the car. Glancing up at the clear blue sky, he gave a grunt of satisfaction as he climbed into the car, slammed the door shut, before starting the engine and exiting the premises.

Annie was just arriving as he drove through the gate. Giving her a wave he set off on the journey to Wragby.

Billings, who was waiting outside his gate waiting for Laxton, climbed into the car with a, 'Morning boss.'

Laxton replied with a nod of his head before setting off for Lincoln.

Wilberton was waiting for them in his office. After the obligatory mugs of coffee had been brought in by the young WPC, they settled down to the job in hand.

'Now then Robert, as you know three of the couples that were involved in the illegal adoption of the four children will be coming in today; at the same time the children's parents will also be here.' He paused as he picked up his coffee and took a drink, then carried on.

'Rebecca Malling has informed us that she will be attending her adopted parents' funeral today and won't be able to attend. As she and her mother Mrs Watling have already been reconciled, they don't need to be here; two of the other three that were abducted when they were children will hopefully also be united with their parents.'

'It's going to be awkward regarding the Bennings and the Rothmans,' Laxton said.

Wilberton gave a nod of his head in agreement; there was a sombre look on his face as he told the inspector, 'We'll have to tread carefully as we go about explaining the situation to them.'

He checked his watch.

'Mmm,' he mumbled, a thoughtful expression on his face as he informed them, 'it's quarter to ten. It won't be long now before they are here.'

'What about Miller and Wooding, have you heard anything about them?' enquired Laxton, leaning forward, his elbows resting on his knees.

'We've received a message informing us that both them and their wives have been arrested and charged with abduction.'

At that moment the young police woman came in and took the empty mugs away. Wilberton addressed her as she turned to leave. 'Tell Sergeant Bellows that I want a word with him will you Constable?'

A few seconds later Bellows came into the chief's office.

'Yes Chief, what do you want to see me about?'

'When the families arrive can you take them into the reception room and make them comfortable?' Wilberton instructed him.

After twenty minutes of discussing different aspects of the case Bellows informed them that all the couples involved had arrived.

The chief inspector, followed by Laxton and Billings, entered the spacious reception room and seated themselves at a table; there was a serious expression on Wilberton's face as he confronted the group of people who were being directed to seats in front of him at the rear of the room. He held a sheet of paper in front of him which he was carefully studying. After they had settled down, he looked up from the paper and addressed them in a serious tone of voice.

'First of all let me say that I'm sure that what has happened wasn't in my opinion done deliberately by the couples who were involved in the adoptions.'

He paused for a moment and pulled at his bottom lip as he thought over carefully what he should say next. Then, as if suddenly making his mind up he told them that his job was to put things right and hopefully that was what he was going to do.

'Now as we finish dealing with all the families

involved, would you please wait in the outer office? There will be a few things to square up,' he told them officiously before carrying on.

'First of all will Mr and Mrs Batley come forward?'

Dorothy and Norman Batley, who had been sat at the rear, got to their feet and approached the table where the officers were sat.

'Now Mr and Mrs Allinson please?' he requested.

Arthur and Lilian Allinson took up a position beside the Batleys, Michael followed suit and stood beside them.

Laxton, who had been stood by watching the proceedings, got to his feet and walked round the table; he stopped and addressed young Michael. 'Michael, can you take your shoes and socks off please?'

The young man was taken aback by what seemed to him a strange request.

'Why do you want me to take my shoes and socks off for?' he retorted.

'Just do as I say Michael,' said the inspector lowering his voice.

Michael looked at his dad questioningly. Arthur nodded his head.

'Okay!' the young man exclaimed before sitting down on one of the chairs and doing as he was bid.

Laxton looked intently at Michael's two bare feet as if matching them. It was clear to see that one of them was smaller than the other. He turned to the Allinsons and put to them that they had told him that when they first adopted the boy, he told them his surname was Batley.

'That is true,' admitted Arthur Allinson.

'Add to that the fact that the Batleys said that the boy had a slight deformity in one of his feet. This and the matching blood groups make it a certainty that he is the abducted son of the Batleys.'

He turned to the young man, telling him that Dorothy and Norman Batley were his true parents.

Michael, shook his head in disbelief as he turned and looked at his true parents. Tears were forming in his mother's eyes as she in turn, looked him up and down.

'My son, my little boy,' she whispered in his ear, as she reached up, put her arms around his shoulders and hugged him.

There was a strong likeness between the young man and Norman, his true father, who turned to the Allinsons, shook their hands and thanked them for looking after their son.

'We've grown to love him as our own over the years,' Lilian and Arthur told his true parents feelingly.

'I hope my adopted parents won't be charged with abducting me!' exclaimed Michael, turning to the chief inspector, a questioning expression on his face.

Wilberton stroked his chin as he thought over the young man's comments.

'Under the circumstances I don't expect them to be charged,' he assured him with a shake of his head.

It was agreed that in the future the two families would keep in close contact with each other. A few minutes later the happy families walked out of the room together.

William and Jane Rothman had been sat quietly as they listened carefully to what was going on. After the previous couples had left the room they were asked to come forward and stand in front of the table; the chief informed them that they were about to be introduced to the true parents of their adopted daughter Jane, who had tragically died at the age of twelve. After a couple of minutes had gone by, Joan and William Benning were requested to stand beside the Rothmans to whom they were introduced.

'First of all I want to ask a few questions to ascertain who the parents of the young woman Jane are,' Wilberton put to them.

The two couples who were strangers, looked at each other questioningly as the chief inspector told them that the blood samples that had been taken when Jane was in hospital had resulted in a perfect match, although they were not conclusive. He turned to the Rothmans and asked them if the child had told them her name during the time she was with them.

The couple nodded their heads.

'Yes she told us that her name was Margaret Benning.'

They went on to say that they had been informed by the persons that had organised the adoption that the child's parents had died.

William Rothman turned to the couple standing beside them, a solemn expression on his face. 'I'm sorry to tell you that your daughter Margaret passed away eight years ago,' he informed the true parents feelingly.

'What did she die of?' enquired Joan Benning, tears forming in her eyes.

'Leukaemia,' was the reply.

'Did she suffer?' she persisted chokingly.

'Not really,' Jane told her, adding sadly, 'she was quite brave.'

After assuring the Rothmans that they held no animosity towards them and that they were happy to know that their daughter had been in good hands, the two couples were ushered out of the room by WPC Smithson.

Then the chief turned to the two remaining couples, Arthur and Marjory Norwood followed by Michael and Jean Gateland. They were formally introduced by Laxton.

After telling the Gatelands that their blood tests had indicated that they were a match; he then went on to also ask the Norwoods, if they had been told by the girl, her former name.

Arthur Norwood informed them that the girl had told them that her name was Caroline Gateland and that they had continued calling her by the same Christian name. 'We were also informed that her parents were dead,' he added.

Jean Gateland, who had been listening carefully to what was being said, addressed the chief, her voice breaking with emotion. 'That surely proves that the girl is my daughter.'

'It certainly does look that way Mrs Gateland.'

'Do you have any photographs of your daughter?' interjected Laxton.

'Yes, in fact I've got one here,' she said, opening her handbag, adding a little excitedly, 'it was taken about a week before she went missing. I always carry it with me.'

Taking it out of her handbag she handed it to the inspector, who in turn took a look at the well-worn photograph. He handed it to the Norwoods. There was a deep intake of breath from Marjory Norwood as she observed the little girl on the photograph.

'That's our Caroline,' she gasped, a look of disbelief on her face.

Wilberton addressed the two couples.

'It seems to me that the best thing you can do is get together and plan how you can continue to give this young woman a happy and contented life.'

At that moment Bellows came through the door; he was accompanied by a young, pretty, blonde-haired woman.

'Caroline Norwood,' he announced as he led her towards the two couples that were standing in front of the inspector.

The young woman had a perplexed, questioning look on her face as she saw that her mum was upset.

'What's the matter Mum?' she enquired feelingly.

Marjory put her arms around her and gave her a hug before turning to Jean and Michael Gateland and telling her in a soft voice, 'Caroline, these are your real parents.'

The young woman's blue eyes were wide with shock as she took in the unexpected revelation that the couple, who were standing in front of her, were, indeed her true father and mother.

'My real parents?' she repeated falteringly, a look of disbelief on her face as she turned and looked Michael and Jean Gateland in the eyes.

'Yes it's true my dear,' Jean mumbled, her speech

almost overcome by the deep feelings that were almost bursting out of her heaving breast as she added, 'you are the daughter that we lost all those years ago.

There were tears forming in her eyes as she reached out and gave her daughter an affectionate squeeze. She turned to the Norwoods, who had been looking on at the remarkable meeting of the girl's former true family.

'I and my husband would like to thank you from the bottom of our hearts for showing love and kindness to Caroline and for caring for her all these years.'

'We loved her as if she were our own daughter. It's been a pleasure and a comfort to have helped in bringing her up,' replied Arthur Norwood, his voice full of emotion.

Caroline stepped forward, her arms outstretched as she embraced both mothers.

There were tears in her eyes as she addressed her adoptive parents.

'You are the only ones that I've known as my parents. The love and care that you have shown me really was something special.'

She paused for a moment before turning to Michael and Jean Gateland.

'As you can see I have a love for the mum and dad that I've had all these years. Now that I've discovered that you are my true parents, it won't alter my feelings for them. I know that I shall have to get to know you more in the future.'

At that point Laxton stepped in; he could see that it was becoming awkward for the young woman.

'You will have all the future to work out your relationships,' he advised them, adding a little sharply, 'the chief wants you to join the others in the outer office.'

A few seconds later the chattering group was gathered together in readiness for Wilberton to address them. He held his hands up indicating for them to be quiet.

'First of all I must inform you that the people who were behind this crime of abduction have been arrested and they are being held in custody prior to them being charged.'

He paused for a moment to let what he had told them sink in, then carried on.

'The couples who took in the children will probably have to show themselves in court at the appropriate time.'

Arthur Norwood stepped forward, a belligerent expression on his face.

'Why should we have to go to court? We haven't committed a crime.'

There was a loud grunt of assent from the group.

'I know you haven't committed a crime!' exclaimed the chief, going on to explain: 'You may be needed as witnesses.'

'How will we know when we are needed to be there?' Norwood persisted.

'You will be given plenty of notice,' explained the chief, a little exasperated.

A few minutes later they were all ushered out of the office and sent on their way with a, 'You will all be notified in due course.'

Wilberton gave a deep sigh of relief as he led Laxton and Billings to his office.

'I'm pleased we got that lot sorted out,' he told his two officers as they took a seat.

'What about the Fulbeks, do you reckon they will be charged as accessories?' Laxton put to the chief.

'I should think so, but as they have treated the children with care, I reckon they will probably come out of it with a suspended sentence.'

Laxton looked at his watch; it was just coming up to two o'clock. He turned to his young partner.

'It's time we got a bite to eat Alan,' he suggested as he got to his feet.

Bidding the chief farewell, Laxton and Billings walked out of the office and made their way down the road to one of the well frequented fish and chip cafés.

After a satisfying meal they sat for a while drinking a mug of coffee and going over the rudiments of the case in hand. Over an hour had gone by when Laxton turned to his partner and informed him that it was now three o'clock and that it was time they were getting back. The young man jumped to his feet and followed the inspector out of the café and back to the police station. Walking into Wilberton's office, they were told there was nothing pending and that their services would not be needed for the rest of the afternoon. The inspector smiled his thanks, then with a, 'See you tomorrow Chief,' the two left.

Laxton looked up at the clearing sky as they approached the car.

'It looks as though it's going to be a nice evening after all,' he said to his partner as he climbed behind the steering wheel and drove off.

After an uneventful twenty minutes they arrived at Alan's home. His mother, cutters in hand, was doing a bit of pruning as they pulled up. She looked up at her son as he climbed out of the car and approached her; she had a look of surprise on her face.

'You are early Alan,' she told him.

'Yeah Mum, the chief didn't need us any more today.'

'You'd better finish pruning this bush, while I get your dinner on,' she instructed him as she passed him the cutters.

'Aw Mum,' he groaned as she turned to leave him after giving the inspector a smile and a farewell wave.

Laxton had a broad grin on his face as he waved back and drove away.

The sun was shining from a predominantly blue sky as he turned off the main highway and made his way across the undulating Wold countryside. He drank in the beauty of it. The strains of 'Moon River' sung by Johnny Mathis drifted round the car as he descended the steep hill and entered Old Bolingbroke.

Dougie, one of his neighbours, who was out walking his black Labrador, gave him a wave. Laxton acknowledged him with a smile and a nod of his head before turning into his driveway. Annie was just starting his dinner as he walked through the door.

'You are early Mr Laxton, I'm afraid your meal won't be ready for a while yet,' she told him a little concernedly.

'Don't worry Annie,' he told her, giving her a pat on her shoulder as he walked past her on his way to the bathroom for a shower, adding, I'm not ready for it yet. I've had a meal at two o'clock.' He checked his watch before telling her, 'That's less than three hours ago.'

After his shower he went into the lounge and spread himself out on the settee and waited for his dish of lamb chops and roast potatoes that Annie was preparing for him.

As he was eating the meal, he went through the day's events in his mind.

He was broken out of his reverie by Annie bidding him goodbye. He raised his hand in acknowledgement and carried on with his meal. After a lazy evening he had an early night in preparation for what may be in front of him tomorrow.

Wilberton was sat at his desk, a sheet of A4 in his hand as Laxton and Billings walked into his office and took a seat in front of him. There was a serious expression on his face as he addressed them. 'I've just had word from the Super; he's informed me that the two chief suspects that we have in custody i.e. Robert Miller and Thomas Wooding, have opened up.'

He paused for a moment as a smiling WPC Smithson came through the door carrying a tray with three coffees on it and placed it on the desk; Wilberton returned the smile and nodded his head as she turned and left the office. Each of them reached out and picked up a mug of coffee. The chief, after taking a sip of the hot drink, carried on with his interpretation of the document.

'They have admitted that they are involved with other similar abductors of small children all over Europe; it seems that, over the years other children have gone missing while on holiday with their parents. A number of arrests have been made and the investigation into the case is still ongoing.'

The chief sat back in his chair, his arms folded.

'What now Chief?' enquired Billings.

Wilberton turned to the young man, explaining to him, 'I reckon they will be duly charged and eventually brought in front of the beak.'

Six weeks later the case came up. Laxton and Billings attended the hearing. The different families that had been involved in the abductions were also there. The inspector was pleased to see them conversing in a friendly manner as he and his partner approached the court. Laxton could see that Billings was a bag of nerves as they climbed the stone steps and entered the imposing building; he leaned over and told him in a low voice, 'Pull yourself together Alan. It will be all over soon.'

A couple of hours later the judge summed up the case:

'This is a very serious case of child abduction. Loving families have been deprived of their rightful possession and the pleasure of raising their children. Although the children themselves have had years of happiness with their so-called adoptive parents, who, incidentally I commend for the way they have shown their love, it still doesn't alter the fact that the natural parents have had many years of happiness stolen from them just for the lure of money.'

He paused for a moment before turning his attention to the perpetrators of the crime. First of all, the Fulbeks. Martin Fulbek was sentenced to three years imprisonment for aiding and abetting; his wife Janet was given a two-year suspended sentence. He paused again before turning to the main culprits, Ronald and Helen Miller and Thomas and Emily Woodings who were equally complicit in the abduction of the children. He dipped his bewigged head and scrutinised them over the rim of his thick-rimmed glasses.

'Your actions in abducting these children solely for monetary gain have caused unimaginable heartbreak to four families. The only course I can take is to penalise you with a heavy sentence.'

The two men looked straight ahead, stony-faced. The women sobbed gently into their handkerchiefs as the judge paused for a moment as he shuffled through the papers on his desk. After a few seconds he raised his head and eyed both couples for a few seconds before telling them unfeelingly, 'Ronald and Helen Miller and Thomas and Emily Wooding, I am sentencing each of you to be detained for ten years at her majesty's pleasure.'

He straightened up and banged the gavel to bring the proceedings to a close.

END

Printed in Poland
by Amazon Fulfillment
Poland Sp. z o.o., Wrocław